THE FILLED IN SPACES

Michael Overa

Published by Unsolicited Press.
Copyright © 2017. Michael Overa.
All Rights Reserved.
ISBN: 978-1539526957

This book is dedicated to those still trying to learn how to care for the writers they love. Please continue to overlook the fact that we talk about made up people as though they are real. Without you, books like this wouldn't exist. And, besides that, all of our terrible vices would be far worse without you. Just keep telling us everything will be okay.

Stories

Fix	1
Oxygen	23
Inevitable	40
Evidence of Life	53
Second Run	72
The Filled in Spaces	82
We Live Here Now	89
They Say	99
Potential Truth	103
Off the Tracks	107
This Endless Road	125
Acknowledgements	155

Fix

I can hear Pockets and those two kids talking out there in the front room, picking at a frozen pizza, and I know that their feet are kicked up on a coffee table so battered that Goodwill had thrown it away. Duct tape holds one of the legs on, and someone has tagged it with paint pen – looping yellow and orange letters like bubbles or puddles. The ashtrays overflow with stubbed out cigarettes. Nubs of candles soft flicker on the table. I make my way out into the room. I'm groggy and coming down. A girl that I don't know sits against the old radiator reading. The curtains brush back and forth above her, letting in little bits of orange streetlight. Her head is shaved except for bleached bangs that hang in greasy threads against her forehead.

The girl wears a pair of cutoff cargoes over torn fishnets. I touch Pockets on the shoulder. He reaches up and puts his hand over mine and smiles, but goes on talking, not moving his hand and not looking up at me. I give up on Pockets and walk over to the girl. She folds her book closed, keeping her place with one finger, and looks over at me to ask for a cigarette. Says her name's Dee.

"I'm not going to fuck you," she says.

"It's a cigarette," I scrunch down beside her. "I'm Loner."

"My blood itches."

"Even Pockets is short."

"I might fuck for a fix," she is scratching her arms.

"SoCo might be holding," I ash my cigarette out the window.

I walk back to the bedroom and stuff my things back down into my pack. When I come back into the hallway I can see Dee waiting for me by the front door, drumming her hands on her thighs. The hallway outside the apartment is graffiti crowded and the drywall at the top of the stairs has been kicked in, exposing wires and copper pipes. The plan is to head down towards the Blade to cop. As we walk downhill towards the water and she tells me that she was in LA last, and that her big brother had fixed her for the first time so that she could escape her step-dad, who'd taken her virginity. At fourteen, she says, she left the house for the last time and went to New Orleans to find her brother.

"Kid he was traveling with knifed him," she says, "somewhere in the Quarter."

A block ahead I can see a hobo rocking back and forth on the stoop of an old apartment building. I walk up to him and take the forty of beer right out of his hands. Maybe I'm showing off, or maybe I want a drink. I push him down the steps with little more than a nudge, and he curls into a ball and doesn't move. Dee spits on him as I'm wiping the mouth of the bottle clean, and we keep walking, passing the bottle back and forth until it's empty. Dee tosses the bottle at a car on Third and Union, but it falls short and shatters like fireworks in the glow of taillights.

Closer to the market we see two Frat boys having a punching match in an empty parking lot. Their jackets are thrown down on the wet pavement, and the wrestle with each other, tearing at each other's T-shirts and swinging wild. Dee goes up and asks them for a smoke, and while they're looking at her I run past and topple the smaller guy, snag his leather jacket and sprint down the street. When Dee catches up with me a block later we can hear those Frat boys yelling about what fucking trash we are. Their voices echo off of the buildings as we search the jacket. There's a phone and some cash, a pack of cigarettes. We're feeling pretty good from the cheapo beer and I ditch the jacket. I don't want to be caught with something that's going to be a bitch to sell.

The sun's coming up as we hit Pike and walk down First to the Blade smelling salt water and hearing the gulls. Shops are starting to open up and street performers are setting up cardboard signs and portable radios. They're drawing chalk circles on the sidewalks to keep tourists at bay. An older guy stakes claim on a park bench and takes out plastic baggies of colored pencils and a battered sketchpad. This guy is the only person who looks at us as we pass, and I can tell he doesn't think much of us. It doesn't matter anyways, since I know that SoCo will be down here somewhere. For the right price he can hook up some pretty decent H.

We find him standing near a parking garage farther down First near the art museum. We cop enough to last us a few days and pay with the Frat boy's money. I bury the dose in my pack and we catch the 42 towards Georgetown, where I know a place we can fix. There's an abandoned warehouse at the end of the runway, and we can fix there, under the angry hornet engine whine of planes landing at Boeing Field.

The building isn't far from where the bus drops us, and it's early, so there aren't many people around. I hop the fence first and she follows, hanging from the chain link with one hand and pulling my jacket off of the razor wire. It takes a few kicks to get the boards out of one of the windows, and inside the building there are dirty rays of sun passing through gaps in the boards.

We find a little spot on the second floor, near a window that looks down at the street. I fix her first, using my kit. I cook off her dose watching the bubbles swell and pop in the spoon. Black Tar gums up the needle. She winces as the needle goes in, but it only takes a second before her eyes droop and she mumbles nonsense at me while I clean the needle with rubbing alcohol and my lighter. I fix and the ceiling spirals high and distant above me as I lie back at her feet.

We wake up feeling hazy. The building has a musty smell and the air is thick. My kit is spread out on the Crown Royal bag I keep it in. There are a few syringes lying on the metal mint container, my spoon – all the other bits and pieces. I pick up what's left of the H we bought from SoCo and figure it will last us until we can find a little more money. I look at her and think about how the drug brings people closer together, even if it's only momentary. Sober we wouldn't cross the street to piss on each other.

After a few hours we walk down to the Jules Mae Saloon and trade the Frat kid's phone to a biker for a little bit of cash. After seven or eight shots of bourbon we head back to the warehouse. It's about closing time and it's rained at some point during the day, slicking the asphalt to a reflective sheen. I slip as I drop down on the other side of the fence and fall flat on my ass laughing as Dee drops down beside me. The sound of bikers gunning their engines cuts the air as single headlights trace over us and across the front of the abandoned building. Back on the second floor of the building we lay laughing on the floor. And then it's a drunken, fumbling fuck. Her hands up against the brick wall, by a gap in the boards. The only light is the light from the airport sneaking through the gaps in the boards. I run my hands over the crooked wings tattooed on her shoulder blades, my fingers catch in her necklaces. Needle punches and cigarettes along her forearms as she reaches towards me, naked, unashamed.

When we're sober enough we fuck on the bare mattress in the back room at Pockets' apartment. Out of nowhere it's July and we've been in town over a month, squatting in Georgetown when we want to be alone, and hanging out at the beach around bonfires with the freaks down there. Those fuckers couldn't avoid the pigs or the railroad bulls if their lives depended on it. They get picked up for mouthing off or get caught carrying kitchen knives and shanks fashioned from some post-prison-know-how.

Abscesses, ODs, and withdrawals are part of our lives. At least once a week someone ends up in a bad way while hanging out at Pockets' and I end up dropping most of them off at the Harborview ER. Junkies who've turned into the walking dead, slumped against me as I drag them through the sliding glass doors and dump them in the hard plastic seats. Pockets' can't deal with all that noise. His partner OD'd a few years back, and since then the place has gone downhill. People get so out of it that all you can do is try to keep them moving. It takes Dee and I almost an hour one night to drag this kid, Gumby, five blocks down to the Burger King. When we got back to the apartment I could smell his sweat on me, and I had to rinse his vomit off of my shoes under the shower. Dee is sitting there, on the edge of the bathtub watching me.

"Who's going to take care of you?"

"He'll be fine," I say shutting off the water and shaking water off my shoes. "Who gives a fuck about him?" She stands up and wraps her arms around my waist. It's the most tender moment we've shared.

"I mean," she says, "what about you?"
"Nothing's going to happen to me," I say.

Walking down Broadway, dodging people, Dee keeps falling behind me. I'm moving pretty fast because we need to get to the Central District to score. I stop and wait for Dee, and when she catches up I take her pack off her shoulders and sling it over mine. I start walking again, Dee beside me, and she reaches over and curls her fingers through mine. I guess we must look like an almost normal couple, even though I don't give a fuck about normal.

We score and fix, and by that evening we're spare changing in front of Dick's. If we're lucky someone will hand us a burger, wrapped up in its orange foil. Most of the gutter punks hang out in front of Dick's with cardboard signs, squatting in lines and clusters that make people on the sidewalk catch a wide berth. Like water flowing around a rock.

You get off of the West Coast and you can find some real white shit, pricey, but you buy from dealers that sell to Weekend Warriors who think that they can chase the dragon and not get hooked. They think they got something we don't. Some superhuman bullshit strength. Guys in business suits freebase off of aluminum foil, but wouldn't know how to shoot up if their life depended on it. Satchel once shot up in a ritzy hotel in LA with some Yuppie who was OD'ing, he had to squeeze the guy's balls to keep him from dying. Next to a Narcon shot it's the best way to keep a guy alive. Nobody wants somebody dying on them.

A lot of fake punks hang out on the drag too – one of the few places we can blend in. As far as I'm concerned they could fuck themselves, these kids with faux-hawks and carefully torn pants. We are near the weekend flea market one afternoon when we see a guy with a cardboard sign that says "free dogs." We walk over to his big red Lincoln, and he has the trunk open and there are three or four pups in this big cardboard box. It seems like Dee might climb into that trunk, and it makes me more than a little nervous. Nervous because I feel like I'm seeing how Dee might have been once. She picks out a dog and names him Buster. He's some kind of mutt, mostly grayish black with pointy ears and cool gray eyes. Later in the afternoon I find a length of rope in a dumpster on Summit and turn it into a leash.

Everyone knows that dogs are an easy way to make money when you're spare changing. Most people will avoid eye contact with you no matter what your sign says. Even if you can get them to laugh or smile when they read your sign they don't want to give you cash. But if you have an animal people feel guilty, they feel like, maybe, the animal doesn't deserve to go hungry. They'll look right past you at the pouting dog, and their heart softens and they go for their wallet.

My brother Trevor lives in West Seattle. He moved out there with his woman a few years before I got back into town, so I knew that I had a safety net if I needed a place to stay. At nineteen I'd been familiar with the circuit for five years – give or take – riding trains down through California and into Texas and New Orleans, sleeping in rattling cars and piss-smelling alleyways. Trevor and I had never really been that tight. We shared a room at one point, but I was pretty young and I don't think that he knew what to do with a little brother who was already smoking and drinking more than he was.

By the time he moved out of the house I was already running with the local punks, skipping class and cutting down to the University District to hang out on 45th drinking forties in the 7-11 parking lot. I guess I'd been a pretty good kid until the divorce, but I couldn't handle it. Mom started drinking more and I think she cared, but it was a tough time for her. I mean, she was a good mom, but she had a lot of shit she was dealing with.

It doesn't matter – it wasn't until I called Trevor a year ago that I found out that she had gotten remarried to some ex-Marine who sounded like he could be a real asshole. The guy liked Trev though. Trev had turned out to be the type of ex-high school football star who goes to church on Sunday and comes home, cracks a beer and watches ESPN for hours. Trev's a good guy, and always has been. He doesn't realize how empty his world is.

    Up on the backside of Capitol Hill there's a place called Volunteer Park. It's not a huge park but it's big enough that you can hide out there, and you can figure that the pigs won't cruise through on any sort of regular basis. Dee and I are out there one day, hanging out in the sun not far from the Asian Art Museum, when I see Satchel making his way towards us. I know him from when I was staying in Portland. He'd been working at a fast food place in the Rose District, and he used to hook me up with free food now and then.

    Buster is lying in the grass nearby with this bored expression on his face as if he's waiting for something to happen. The park was rippled with shadows – the punks stuck to the shade, laying their torn shirts and boots in the grass and sprawling in little groups either on or off the nod. I lean against a tree, my feet dug into the soft, dry dirt. Dee sits nearby sewing a patch of black fabric over the torn knee of her cargo pants with dental floss.

    Satchel sits down and takes off his pack; his light brown Carhartt overalls are held u with a piece of chain that he's turned into a belt. He sits down beside us and digs a little flask of whiskey out of his pack and offers it to us. I like this part of being on the streets. You always run into people you know, and it's like a reunion. I'm happy that they're alive. I lean forward and we hug each other and I introduce him to

Dee, who smiles and keeps sewing in long movements.

"Skank OD'd in Portland last week," he says. "Fixed and that was it. By the time he we realized he was dead it was too late to do anything."

"Fuck." I light a cigarette.

"That's why I had to get out of there," he takes his whiskey back. "I need to cop, you know anyone that's holding?"

"Pockets, down on Bellevue," I say. "If anyone's holding it's him."   Satchel nods and picks up his pack. It's then that I notice that the Docs he's wearing look like Skank's. That's the way the world turns. Death means new boots, a new jacket – or, if you're lucky – a fix. I'm not going to say that it's all silver fucking clouds, but you have to take it all in stride. Junkies like us OD every day and no one gives a shit. Even the people that we used to fix with are going to get over it in less time than it takes to cook off a dose. You build up a tolerance after seeing your first dozen dead bodies. You put it in a different vein

I'm watching Satchel make his way across the field when Dee stands up and stretches, leaning back with her arms out at her sides. The weight of her studded belt pulls down the edge of her pants a fraction of an inch, and I can see the pale skin of her stomach and the hard ridge of her hips bones.

By early evening the sun is going down and the cars are starting to thin out on the road. Off and on shouting and barking careens through the trees making the whole place feel hollow. Trees and bushes are clumped in the center of the park, and all around the grass is broken only by a few picnic tables. A little farther up the hill there's a shallow fountain, and not far from that is an old brick amphitheater.

Some of the other punks had left, but Dee and I had decided to stay there for the night. After hearing about Skank I didn't really want to head back to Pockets' place to deal with the noise of people OD'ing and begging for doses and all that shit. Dee pushed her way back into some of the bushes and flattened the underbrush down with a piece of cardboard. We fucked there in the bushes, our pants around our ankles, and the cardboard sliding back and forth under us.

We fix and fall asleep, and the next thing I know I'm waking up in the silent early morning and I notice that Buster is gone. His leash is coiled in my pocket and when I reach over to where he was laying on my jacket the leather is warm. I sit up and pull on my boots and jacket. There's dew on everything. It's cold and damp and a bright sun is rising and hanging out there on the horizon – making things seem colder than they actually are. When I don't see Buster I nudge Dee with my boot and she wakes up not having to ask me what is going on. She realizes right away that Buster is gone. She tugs on her hoodie and shoves her hands into the kangaroo pouch, her shoulders hunched up and her hair stuck to her forehead.

    Dee takes off through the bushes without putting on her shoes. She sets off at a sprint through the trees, and leaving branches vibrating behind her. I grab her shoes and our gear and head out after her. When I catch up with her she is sitting on the low edge of the amphitheater smoking. I drop our gear beside her and set her shoes on the ground in front of her.

    "Can't find him," she says without looking at me.

    "He's around somewhere."

    "I don't think we'll find him."

    She pitches her cigarette butt into the grass and stands up, bending over to put on her shoes.

    "I need to fix," she says.

    For weeks, well into early August, we split our time between the parks and Pockets'. More than a few times we stayed on the beach at Golden Gardens, sleeping tucked back in the long grass; building bonfires out of driftwood and watching the tide go in and out. We fixed behind the dunes and lay down to let the water wash over our ankles, the sand sifts into the seams of our pants. Skin stained with salt and sun, boots tucked back behind us in the pebble scrabble and weeds. It was a bit of a hike back to Highway 99, but once we hit that drag we could usually find somewhere to cop.

When we had cash we stayed at a no-tell-motel set back between the dive bars and car lots. The carpet in those places is always a disgusting color: green or brown or mustard yellow. The furniture is perpetually outdated. Bad paintings – prints really – of mountains and sunsets hang on the walls in those places. A night in a motel means a shower, a real toilet, and a decent bed.

Around that time, I start to think about getting Dee another dog, but after a while not much matters except for the next fix. Besides, I know that it isn't any kind of love, what we have between us. A junky, like me, can only really fall in love with the drug. Now and then, I think that I can see what the world would be like if Dee and I finally got clean and made it off of the streets. Then reality sets in and I realize that we don't know each other without the drug. I mean, fuck, what would we do for fun, and what would we have to talk about?

Regardless of whatever the two of us feel or don't feel for each other, both of us are about ready to get out of town. The town's about tapped out as far as we know, and if we can scrape together some cash we can catch a train down into Cali and spend fall and early winter somewhere warm. I call Trevor from a payphone outside of Dick's and I tell him I'm in town. I tell him I just got in, and that I need some work so that I can get myself off the streets. It's an easy lie to tell because he wants to believe me. Trevor's running some kind of landscaping gig lately, his own business he tells me.

"I can probably use an extra set of hands," he says. "If you want work."

"Okay," I say.

"I'm not going to give you a handout."

"I'm not looking for one."

We arrange things and Trevor picks me up a few days later and drives me back out to West Seattle in his yellow Toyota pickup. The place that they are renting out there on Fauntleroy makes the motels look like a fucking paradise in comparison. The house is one of those low-slung places with bars on the windows, and the whole place has this sour smell. Not a strong smell, but it's there, underneath the smell of fresh paint and the spaghetti his woman cooked for us. I can tell by the way that she looks at me that she doesn't want me there. She's the type of girl that's happy with working her eight-hour shift at the beauty salon giving old ladies perms and gluing on fake nails and all that shit. She sees me come in and she looks at me like she wants to call the cops.

We eat and his woman goes to bed. I think that I can hear her lock the bedroom door behind her. Trevor and I sit at the kitchen table and he cracks a beer and sits down across from me.

"So, how are you, man?" he asks.

"Trev, look. No bullshit. I just need some cash then I'll be out of your hair."

"You really trying to get clean?"

"I just told you I was."

Trevor lets the whole thing go. Thing about these type of conversations is that people think that they can help us out – they think they know better and they got everything figured out. I can name twice as many things that's wrong with his lifestyle than he can name that are wrong with mine. Other thing is, people always want to believe a junky. They say it's the junk talking, all that sort of thing. Hell, if I can play that card, I'll fucking play it.

Trevor makes a little bed for me on the couch, and I crash there that night. Once he goes to bed I fix and send myself off into dreamland.

I wake up to Trevor shaking my shoulder. We load some gear into his pickup and drive out to a house overlooking the ferry terminal all the way down at the end of Fauntleroy. We peel the grass back from the yard, throw bits of sod into the back of his truck, and spend most of the day raking, leveling, and backfilling the yard. I don't know if we could cut more of a contrast: Trevor tall, rippling with muscles, tan. Me: thin and pale with needle punches in my arms. For the most part it was like old times, before I first left town, back when we did odd jobs for a little pocket change. Late in the afternoon, as shadows stretch out across the lawn Trevor straightens up, and leans on his shovel, wiping sweat from his forehead.

"Hey, man, you need anything?"

"I'm good," I say. It takes me a minute to realize he's not talking about water or a break.

"I mean, anything."

"I'm good," I repeat.

"Sarah found this place downtown. Stone-something-or-other."

"Stonewall," I say. "I know the place. It's a methadone clinic."

Trevor yanks his shovel out of the ground and looks around at the yard. There is dust coating his jeans, and he pulls off his leather gloves and slaps them against his thighs. Trevor checks his watch and says it's about quitting time, and I help him load the shovels and sod cutter and rakes and hoes into the back of his truck. While Trevor talks to the homeowner I tie everything down, making sure that the sod won't fly out of the back. All I can think about is getting back to town and fixing. My blood feels razor edged in my veins, my mouth tastes coppery and dry. If Trevor notices me shifting around in the seat he doesn't say anything.

The radio pumps country music, and I'm almost certain that I'll be out of my mind by the time he pulls into the 76 Station and runs inside to get beer and chew. No one is around in the parking lot, and I dig my kit out of my bag, cook off a quick dose and fix there in the passenger seat. I rub at the dot of blood pooling on my arm and slapped the veins. I get everything put away by the time he comes back out a few minutes later, but either he thinks I'm tired, or doesn't realize that my eyes are half-closed and my body like a ragdoll.

Back at his place his girlfriend has dinner waiting for us. Salad, bread, pasta. Trevor cracks a beer and sits down at the table to eat. My eyes lock onto the way his hand curls around the sweating can. I feel myself lean forward on the table, numb and a little anxious. I try not to move. Moving will make it more apparent that I'm high. I can feel their eyes on me – I can feel their knowing. I sit there while they eat.

When they are done Trevor fills a Ziploc bag with pasta and wraps some bread in tin foil and hands the whole thing to me. The high is getting thin. I press the food into my pack and I can hear plates clattering in the kitchen as we walk out to his truck again. I don't bother to say goodbye to his woman.

The ride back is quiet. The sun is going down and as we drive over the West Seattle Bridge I can see the low buildings and warehouses, and all the gray reality of the Industrial District. The radio plays but I'm not listening. Trevor glances over at me at intervals, but can't come up with the words to say whatever he's thinking. I try to call up some memories of us as kids, but nothing really comes to mind. In reality, I guess I don't want to think about it at all. There doesn't seem to be any reason to dwell on childhood and growing up. That shit's so far behind us, and it's not who I am anymore. Why make it syrupy?

Trevor pulls onto Broadway and I'm already looking to see if there's anyone I know on the streets. I pull my pack up onto my lap as we roll into the Dick's parking lot and Trevor punches the E-break into place. He leans hard towards the door and digs into his folded, battered wallet. He opens it, peers inside, and peals out some bills.

"Look," he says, "I'm going to give you more money than you earned for landscaping. But, it's not a handout."

I take the cash from him.

"Thanks," I say pushing the door open.

"Hey," he says, "fuck. Take care of yourself."

There's no real way that you can respond to something like that: a big, tanned all-American-boy about to cry. I slam the door and put on my pack, tucking the cash down into my front pocket. I am already planning how Dee and I will get out of town. I'm thinking about getting some H and hanging out at Pockets' for the next day, and leaving for Cali tomorrow night. I'm not sure where to find her so I try Pockets' first and then the Park. Around midnight I curl up in the bushes near the same spot we slept the night before Buster ran away. I wake up the next afternoon and walk down to Dick's and find some other gutter kids down there who tell me they saw Dee down at the Blade that morning.

Pockets looked surprised to see me at first but his surprise started to look like fear when I heard people fucking in the back room. I don't know why I expect it to be Dee, but it's those two kids that have been staying with him all summer. The boy's dirty white ass is bobbing in the air, and the girl looks over at me with a type of dullness in her eyes.

"Shut the fucking door," the kid says and I turn and walk back towards the living room. Pockets is sitting in there leaning forward in his chair, sweating. About ten minutes pass and I can hear someone laughing in the bathroom. I light a cigarette and look up as Dee walks out of the bathroom with two Weekend Warriors behind her, both of them zipping up their pants. She sees me sitting there against the radiator. She looks at me, and she seems cold and unfamiliar, as if neither of us recognizes each other.

I don't remember standing up, and I don't remember calling her a whore.

"Money is money," one of the men says.

I throw my cigarette at him, and I hit him hard in the mouth and that he hits the wall and stumbles into the bedroom. I'm on him and I'm not expecting much except to be pulled off by the other guy. It's all limbs and grappling and Dee goes to slap me, but instead drags her nails down my cheek, tearing the flesh back. I can feel the warmth on my skin. One of the Weekend Warrior boys spits down on me, and they take off out the front door. I could give a fuck about them. I'm looking up at Dee and I can feel the blood running down my cheek and tickling my neck.

Dee grabs her shit and walks out the front door without saying anything else, leaving the door hanging wide open behind her. The last I see of her is her backpack disappearing down the stairway. I light another cigarette and use my bandana to wipe the blood from my cheek.

"Loner," Pockets says. "Loner, come fix with me."

I walk over and sit on the arm of his chair, fix him with his kit, then fix myself. I almost double my dosage, hoping that it might be enough to send me off into the great nowhere. I nod off leaning against the side of Pockets' chair, his hand dead weight against my scalp.

The city is small, but not so small that you can expect to run into any one on any given occasion – especially if they're trying to avoid you. But avoiding me means that Dee can't fix at Pockets', so she will have to cop down at the Blade, which is fine by me. The parks are another story, and so was Broadway, and every now and then I see her running with some other punks who hang out farther down Broadway in front of the community college.

The scars on my cheeks are already scabbing over, and every time I run my hand over those three distinct gashes I try and figure out where I went wrong with her. I should have kept it to a fuck. Somewhere in there I started to depend on her for the little things: someone to be around me. Someone to fix with and sometimes talk to.

Near the end of the summer I decide to head down to Portland. Rumor has it that Dee has headed off to New Orleans. Satchel, always the bearer of bad news, was the one that told me. We ran into each other, Satchel and I, in the Pearl District, where I'd been hustling for spare change. We walked along the river and he told me that he'd heard that Dee had OD'd a while back while turning tricks in a motel somewhere near Austin, Texas.

"Know you had a thing," he says.

"Forever ago," I say.

"Cook off the gear," he says. "Forget about all that shit."

We've scored from a connection I have downtown, and we make our way back to a junkyard I've been staying in for the past couple days. We huddle in the rusted out hulk of an old vee-dub bus. It isn't a bad place to stay, and there's never anyone around to bother me. Satchel finds a vein and his head thumps back against the metal shell of the bus. I sit there, slapping my arms – my belt cinched down around my arm, puckering the flesh. I search for a vein. I cook without bothering to look at Satchel. I close my eyes. Let the drug take over. Let the world slip away. My head drops to my chest. Forget it, a voice inside my dreaming me says. Forget it.

Oxygen

Over the running commentary of the Dodger's game I can hear the clickgasp of his oxygen tank, pushing air down his throat. We are sitting in the mismatched recliners, angled towards the TV, the chessboard is on the table between us. Frank leans over on his thin arms and moves a rook. He plays black, he always plays black, he says it's just as much his team as the Dodgers are.

He's winning again.

I hold up my empty beer can but Frank shakes his head – a little twitch for no – the oxygen tubes waggling against his cheeks. I open the refrigerator and want to climb inside of it. The heat makes everything uncomfortable, even with Frank's oscillating fan pushing around warm air.

"That bum," he says, "you call that a fast ball, you bum?"

I hold the beer can to my forehead and then to the back of my neck, and set the empty beside the sink. I crack the beer and set in on the table next to the chessboard. I wonder if it matters where I move. I stare at the pieces, and Frank stares at the TV. Without looking over at me he asks me am I going to play or what.

"I'm thinking," I say.

"Thinking. This guy. Think away, buddy-boy."

Clickgasp.

The inning ends and Frank looks over at the board.

"That's your move? All that time you think and think, and this is your move?"

When we first met she and I had both done some bad things. Nothing too terrible – but she hadn't stolen or really lied to anyone other than her mother – and then I showed up and she started lying more. Those lies were mostly about me, and I guess I should have felt guilty about that, but I didn't. I'd done worse than she had. I'd done a few months in the Juvie detention center, and had a little bit of a record with the local cops. Shoplifting, destruction of property, trespassing, that sort of thing. No one cares about that shit. That's just kid stuff, anyways.

We met during one of the first weeks of summer when the elevator broke for the umpteenth time. I was standing there with bags full of groceries—some for me, some for Frank — slamming the metal door on the elevator. Bangbang, bangbang, and I looked up and she was standing there. If she had been scared at first, now she was just amused. She was shaking her head at me and smiling and finally she said out loud that she figured the thing was broken.

"If it wasn't before, it is now," I said, "What floor?"

Turns out she lived on the floor beneath me and Frank, and so we kept each other company up the stairs. She told me her name was Karen, and that she lived with her moms and her grandmoms, and that maybe I should knock on the door sometime to see what she was up to. I carried the rest of the stuff up to Frank's place. He was standing in the kitchen making a sandwich. He asked me what took so long and told me to open us a couple of beers.

My apartment's two doors down from Frank's. Between us there is an old lady who lives with her garbage man son who has a constant glaze of sweat and thick black hair like patches of crab grass. There's a lady on the other side of the hall who leaves her TV playing for hours and hours and hours, the volume always turned up too high. You can hear her TV at eight AM when she turns it on to watch the morning talk shows.

One day, Frank has enough, he walks into the hall, dragging his tank behind him. He pounds on her door, shouts for her to turn it the hell down, for god's sake. The lady calls the cops, and I come out into the hall to find Frank leaning against the wall talking to a cop as the old lady stands in the doorway of her apartment with her arms crossed.

"Ma'am, please turn your TV down," says the cop.

"I been telling her that all freakin' day," says Frank.

"Please, ma'am, turn the TV down,"

The old lady shuffles back into her apartment and I hear the TV go down to an almost reasonable volume.

"For you she turns it down," Frank says.

I pass Karen on the front steps of the apartment about a week after we first met. She's standing out there, smoking a cigarette, and watching the traffic pass on Gleeson Street. I sit down on the steps beside her, and she looks down at me. The street smells like exhaust, and the garbage that is beginning to pile up along the curb.

"The grocery man," she says, and sits down next to me, "how are you grocery man?"

We talk for a bit and I tell her I have to get going – which is true, I'm supposed to be at the pizzeria in a little less than twenty minutes, and the bus ride usually takes me at least fifteen. I say I'll see her around, and she says, yeah, maybe I will. I force myself not to look over my shoulder at her, and all the way to work I have the image of her burned into my mind. Her head tilted to the left, her eyes rolled up towards the streetlights -- that smooth stream of smoke gray from her lips.

The first night we have sex is after the Fourth of July party on the roof of the building. I've gone up there with Frank, and it seems like almost everyone is up there. The TV lady, the old lady and her Neanderthalic son; Karen her moms, her grandmoms, her sister, and two nieces. Even the landlord is up there, with her sullen partner, who sulks by the chips and watches the fireworks without oohing and ahhing like the rest of us. Someone has brought up a card table and a couple bags of chips, and I've hauled up a cooler full of beer and soda.

Karen is wearing a white windbreaker, and holds one of her nieces propped on her hip as the fireworks bang and snap. She smiles at me, and I stand next to her even though I can't think of anything to say. We watch the fireworks exploding in the distance, glittering back from the water. People on other roof tops shout and wave at us, and we make guesses at how drunk they are, or who will fall off of the roof first.

Frank is sitting in an old chaise lounger, his legs looking thin on the fabric.

"The great American holiday," he says, "celebrate what you can eat, drink, and blow up."

Frank tells me my problem with chess is I don't think ahead. He says I've got to think ahead, but it never made sense to me. Even when I try to think ahead, Frank does something that throws off my plan, and I'm back at square one.

I've brought him pie from the pizzeria, and the box sits on the coffee table, grease staining the box and the table. His mostly uneaten slice sits on the arm of his chair and he twists a paper towel over and under his fingers as he thinks about his next move.

I'm not sure when he eats, if ever. His grocery list seems to get smaller and smaller. Today I've brought him a gallon of OJ, a couple of cans of soup, and a few TV dinners.

I met Frank one afternoon while I was moving into my apartment. This was about a year ago.

"Hope you're no junky like the last guy," he said. I told him I wasn't. I told him not to worry, that I wouldn't bother him.

"Quiet, he says," Frank sized me up, "Well just don't bother me buddy-boy,"

The week after I moved in he knocked on my door and asked me if I wouldn't mind running to the store to pick up some things for him. I told him he was bothering me, and he looked at me hard for a second and told me to go fuck myself, then handed me a twenty and a short list of groceries. Since then I guess we just got along. I bring him groceries and he lets me drink his beer, and he tries to teach me how to play chess. I wonder how long he has been shut up in his apartment, not wanting to go out – not entirely able to go out. The more I hang out in his apartment I realize that the phone never rings.

Every other Wednesday a nurse named Elsa comes by to pick Frank up for his doctor's appointments. I'm glad this is one errand I don't have to run. It's gotten to the point that I forget about the oxygen tank and the stacks of prescriptions on the coffee table.

Elsa is a solid looking young blond with a steady smile and something good about her – like a nun or a kindergarten teacher. I met her the first time as they made their way down the flights of stairs, he had one arm looped through hers, and the other on the railing. She carried his oxygen tank, holding the bottle in its nylon-carrying pouch, and he walked with one hand on the railing, steadying himself as they made their way down, down the three flights. The two of them paused on the stairs as I'm made my way up to my place after work.

"Hey kid," Frank says, "freaking appointment."

"I thought maybe you were being arrested again,"

"More cops were like her I'd be begging to go to jail," he says and she smiles.

I was still in my work clothes, and I think it must have been one of those long winter months with long days, because I remember it being pretty cold and dark outside, although it must have only been late afternoon. Frank was sitting in his chair and Elsa was sitting on the coffee table, Frank's foot propped on her knee as she clipped his toenails. He'd made a joke about getting a pedicure, and even from the kitchen I could see that his feet were as yellow as a smoker's stained teeth.

"You're the pizza guy," she'd said, smiled, clipped.

I can't ask him much more than how he is. I don't want to know about his doctor appointments and the other bullshit that he has to deal with – and I figure he probably doesn't want to talk about it either. The have the fleeting thought of Frank and Elsa having sex. I wonder where he would put the oxygen tank, and what that clickgasp would sound like between the creaking bedsprings.

"Kid," Frank says one night, "if I could I would, the only thing deader than my lungs is the piece of meat between my legs."

Although most of the apartments have the same floor plan, they all seem different. There is something alien and disorienting about standing in someone else's apartment – an apartment that seems to be so familiar in some ways, yet all the decorations and furniture is wrong. This is how it is when I visit Karen for the first time.

We've made plans to go out for the evening, down to the corner bar for a drink and then off to a movie. This is after the Fourth of July, after that first time we slept together. Of course it's been about a week and we really haven't seen much of each other so there is this strangeness in the air of not knowing exactly how to act. We're in that gray area. We don't hold hands and we don't kiss. We don't even really know that much about each other, but we've had this one night that we shared which is lodged in my head. I can imagine her, the image of her naked skin, and the way that her hair fell across her shoulder. These little pictures that I framed behind my eyelids.

Her grandmoms is sitting in the kitchen, on one of those high barstools, chopping vegetables. There is a radio on and I can hear some sort of talk show host taking listener phone calls. Karen is grabbing her things, getting ready to leave, and I am stranded in the kitchen with her grandmoms, who is sweating and chopping and chopping and sweating.

"You're the boy who lives in 318," she says.

"That's me," I say, "one in the same."

"You're friends with that horrible old man that lives alone."

"Frank?" I ask, "He's all right, he does his own thing. He's teaching me how to play chess."

She makes a little sound that makes me think that she doesn't believe me. She chops her vegetables and scoops them into a big bowl.

"You take care of my baby now. I can only assume you know how to be a gentleman."

"Don't you worry," I say, "Don't you worry at all."

Karen comes out wearing this summer dress that shows off her lean legs, tanned and smooth. I'm trying to remind myself that I know her, that I have slept with her, that I have touched and tasted that skin, but it seems so unreal. She smiles at me and touches my arm as she walks past me and kisses her grandmoms' cheek.

"Don't stay up," Karen says.

Her grandmoms makes that noise again.

Fourth of July, just before sunset, Frank asks me to go down to his apartment and bring up some more beer and some salsa that he had down there. He says it as if I don't know it is there, and I smile at him, knowing exactly where those things are. As I'm getting ready to head down there Karen says she'd headed down to use the bathroom and get her jacket. We walk down the stairs and this is the first thing that we've had to a real conversation, and it's still mostly small talk. Neither of us are drunk but we're buzzed. I think that I should offer the use of Frank's bathroom or the bathroom in my apartment so that she doesn't have to go down to her apartment – but then I realize neither bathroom is in good enough shape for a girl to use, let alone one like Karen. I'm still grabbing things from Frank's apartment when she comes back up and knocks on the open door of his apartment.

She comes into the kitchen where I'm putting salsa and chips into a bag to carry up to the roof.

"You don't live here with him do you?" she asks.

"No, my place is a few doors down."

She is walking through the living room looking at the chessboard and the TV and the fan and the pictures that Frank keeps on his walls. Pictures of him fly fishing in Oregon, and pictures of him as a young man. There are a few pictures of his wife, who passed away about five years ago.

"Frank seems like a good guy,"

"He's teaching me to play chess," I say.

"People still play chess?"

"Me and Frank do," I say.

I'm standing in the kitchen and she's wandering closer and there's this magnetism, and I'm hearing Frank's voice in the back of my head, telling me to plan my moves -- to strategize. Karen is leaning against the counter with her arms folded, and I walk over and lean next to her. There's this long silence where it's hard to tell what either one of us are thinking. I can't tell what I'm thinking any more than I can tell what she's thinking.

"What's the worst thing you've ever done?" I ask her.

"I feel most guilty about lying to moms," she says.

"Lying, that's it? Not cheating or stealing?"

"Done that too, a bit. Don't figure it was quite as bad," she says, "you ever do time?"

"A little. Juvie."

She turns and smiles at me, I lean forward and kiss her without thinking any farther in the future.

The old woman down the hall is playing her TV too loud again, and I carry my trash down to the dumpster and stop by Karen's place on the way back up. This is after the Fourth of July, this is after the date, and I knock on the door and one of her nieces answers, opening the door and staring at me before running back down the hallway and shouting to her grandmoms that there is a man at the door. That old grandmoms comes around the corner and looks at me once and tells me that Karen isn't home before shutting the door.

Frank hauls is tank around the apartment, easing himself up out of his chair with both hands. I watch him shuffle down the hall, and enter the bathroom. The linoleum in there is checkered black and white. I stare at the photos he has framed on the wall. I stare at a shadowbox of fishing lures that Frank must have made in his younger days. There are little pieces of yellow paper, type-written words naming the lures. He's in the bathroom for a while and I'm about to go ask him if he's okay when I hear the toilet flush. The door opens and he shuffles back down the hall, finally sitting down in his chair – heavy, and out of breath.

"Even taking a shit winds me," he says, "two packs a day for twenty years. Hauling bricks and lumber. Framing, roofing. And now, now I can't even drop a load without getting winded."

I look down at the chessboard and try to decide if I should move my Bishop or my Rook. Frank tilts his head back against the chair and asks me if I can find something better on TV then the sports highlights.

"What, you want fucking golf?" I ask, "I guess that would be more your speed."

"Shut up and move, you mug."

Karen's skin is like warm sand. She lays on my bed, naked, the sheets covering her partially. She is face down, her arms folded under her head, her face smiling. I lay beside her running my fingers down her back and over her shoulder. Now we have time that we didn't have on the Fourth. Time that means that we can lie here, and that we don't have to worry about her getting back to her apartment.

That first night, after the fireworks, and after everyone else had gone to bed, we went down to my apartment for one last drink.

I made my first move just after I we had sat down on the couch with our sweating bottles of beer. She had been talking, telling a story about her family, when I leaned forward and kissed her. There was a slight hesitation before she surrendered. I took the beer bottle from her hand and set it on the coffee table. There was a scramble of hands and clothing and breathing.

We lie there on the couch, twisted together. I reached across and grabbed my bottle of beer and let the condensation drip onto her skin and she shivered and laughed and leaned up and kissed me.

"I should go," she said, sitting up and gathering her clothes.

I watched her dress and adjust her hair over her shoulders. I pulled on my jeans and walked her to the door.

In August Frank died. I let myself into his apartment late one afternoon after work, and there he was sitting in his chair, his head tilted back to one side. His arms lay on the armrests, his feet were flat on the floor, and he was dead. I set his groceries and his mail on the coffee table and sat down and looked at him. There was a cup of coffee and a half of a bagel on the table.

"Asshole," I said, "you never let me win."

I walked to the refrigerator and put the groceries away and used his phone to call Elsa, whose number was magnated to the fridge. When I told her that Frank was dead she gave me one of those quiet, verbal nods and said she'd be over shortly. I moved through his apartment trying to clean it up a little. I threw away the half of a bagel and washed his coffee cup and plate. I stood there for a long stretch of minutes wondering if I should brush his hair, or arrange him in some way. I could maybe find a copy of Moby Dick or the Bible. I could put that book in his hands, maybe using his finger to mark a page somewhere near the end. But I didn't want to touch him. I didn't want to move him. Frank had never been much for disguises or appearances.

His watch was still ticking on his wrist, and I thought how strange it was that the little machine should still be going after he died. The oxygen tank sat by his side, the tubes still threaded up over his ears and into his nostrils.

Elsa was calm when she got to the apartment. She told me that she'd already called the coroner and the undertaker, and that she would take care of all of those things. She carried a clipboard in one hand and her purse was slung efficiently over her shoulder. It reminded me of the UPS guy that always has his little clipboard and goes around dropping off packages and having people sign for them.

The coroner and other strangers started to arrive, so I walked down to Karen's apartment and knocked on the door. There was no answer and I went back to my apartment, but I could hear those official people moving out there, talking, exchanging information. Smooth, professional. They were talking to the landlord now; I could hear her gruff voice agreeing and answering questions. I could hear them even over the old lady's TV. I couldn't stay in my apartment; I stood in the hallway for a while, and finally went down to the corner bar to have a drink or two in Frank's honor.

I must have been there for quite a while, because by the time I got up to leave I was pretty far-gone. I'd been drinking cheap beer and whiskey. My head was spinning and I couldn't lie down, so I took a shower and tried to sober up. I let myself sleep in the next day – called in sick to work, and made coffee and showered again and walked over to Frank's apartment. The door was closed and locked. I took his apartment key off of my key ring and slid it under the door, I figured someone would find it whenever they came by to clean the place up

---

I didn't see Karen much after that. It was the end of summer anyways, and I figured our little fling had just about timed itself out. Not long after Frank died she knocked on my apartment at three in the morning. She had brought a case of beer and told me that she was there to cheer me up. She said she knew it must be hard to lose a good friend like Frank.

"Let's just drink," I said, "I don't want to talk about Frank."

"It's okay," she said, "You'll talk about him when you're ready."

I kissed her, just to shut her up, and we had sex on the floor in my living room. Both of us walking away with rug burns and scratches. She left that night before morning. The case of beer sat in my kitchen, and as I finished the beers over the next day or so I set them up on the linoleum floor, two ranks of cans facing each other. I saw her after that, sometimes, always by accident. We passed in the hall or on the stairs, or shared the elevator ride up when the elevator was working. The old lady's TV still plays loud, and the Garbage Man still sweats.

The funeral is a pretty quiet thing. Frank is cremated and his ashes are given to some grieving family that has come down from Oregon. They are unfamiliar, and it is strange to think that they are related to Frank – that in some way they are part of Frank, or part Frank. I keep looking at people and trying to figure out how they're related to him. None of them seem right. The thought of Frank with family is strange. Where the hell were they when he was holed up in his apartment, I ask myself.

A blond woman in her early forties dries her eyes behind her glasses and holds a blue and gray urn. It seemed right to me that Elsa would be there, just on the fringes, smiling softly, and comforting family with little anecdotes about how much she liked Frank. During the Wake I ask Elsa if she can do me a small favor, I tell her I'd like to have the chessboard. She said she'd see what she could do.

About a week after the wake Elsa knocks on my door and hands me paper shopping bag, with the chess pieces rattling loosely against the board.

"He liked you," she says, "I think you brightened his days."

"He was a mean old fuck," I say.

Unexpectedly Elsa breaks into a large smile and gives me a brief hug.

For a while I set it in its box and kept it under the coffee table. In early fall, near my twenty-seventh birthday I took the chessboard out of its box and set up the pieces. I left the white side facing in and Frank's black team facing out, towards the TV. I knew that he wasn't going to show up, and I didn't have anyone else to play me – not that it would have seemed right to let someone else play black.

Inevitable

Sara stands at the kitchen sink rinsing her cereal bowl no longer watching as the water goes from white to milky pearl to clear she is already up on her tiptoes and craning her neck to see over the fence into the neighbor's yard. She shuts off the water and sets her bowl beside the sink, leaning farther forward, pressing her bony hips against the kitchen counter.

"What's he doing?"

The smell of coffee permeates the room, and, behind her at the table Sean folds the newspaper into precise fourths, snapping the pages into place.

"What's who doing?"

When she doesn't answer right away Sean sets the paper gingerly on the table and crosses the room to stand behind his wife, laying his hands on her shoulders. He follows her gaze looking over the fence to where their aging neighbor, Charlie scoops shovelfuls of sod from the yard, creating the ragged edge of a pit. By night it would seem ominous, but by the direct light of day, where everything is revealed in stark reality it seems nearly innocuous.

"Maybe he's digging a pool?"

Sara continues watching but her head moves left to right and left to right.

"Who for?"

"Himself? Who knows?"

For a moment – before he catches himself – Sean is going to ask whether or not Charlie has grandkids.

And then he realizes that she is just as unlikely to know as he is, and that it would, more than likely than not only remind her of the doctor's visit two months back when they had learned that she would never be able to have children. The doctor had used a phrase that stuck in his head like a piece of glass embedded in his palm: Lutean Phase Defect. As he stands behind her now he can't imagine his wife has a defect; she is so healthy and strong. But it's not a phase. It's not something she'll grow out of. And so, with this thought in his head he simply makes a little noise meant to signify he is both perplexed and still interested.

"Maybe the guy is snapping," he says. His hand comes to rest on his wife's belly and she almost immediately covers his hand with hers and half turns towards him, so close he could kiss her.

"Past tense," she says, "has snapped."

Sara turns slightly left and he takes a step back, knowing that she wants to move away from the window and he gives her space, letting her move out into the kitchen.

"Maybe he needs somebody to talk to."

Sean thinks about mentioning that Charlie's wife, Margaret, left only three months ago, but again he remembers that it is too closely in line with the fateful visit to the doctor's office and he thinks better of it.

"Maybe," he says.

"Go talk to him."

"Me?"

"Why not? He could probably use someone to talk to. Maybe it's only because he's lonely."

The thought itself doesn't make any sense to Sean, but he doesn't want to argue. The man is not digging up his once manicured back lawn because he is lonely or because he needs someone to talk to. Maybe he's digging for some as yet unknown purpose. Maybe he's digging and doesn't want a lot of people coming around asking him why.

"Sure, maybe, look I'll talk to him. Just not right now."

Sara gives him a look that says: if not now, when? And already Sean is beginning to cave; before the end of the day he will be standing in his neighbor's mutilated back yard.

At the grocery store Sean buys two steaks, the best that he can find, decent and well marbled. Twice he puts the steaks back and picks them up again. He gathers up a couple ears of corn and baked potatoes. In the beer aisle he peruses the contents of his basket and looks at the variety, struggling to identify what his neighbor might drink. He searches back into his memory to decide what the older man would want, but he can't think of a single instance of seeing the older man with a particular brand or style of beer. Stout is too heavy, and the cheap stuff is too cheap. Then there is IPA and pale ale, and those seem almost too obvious. In the end he settles on something local.

By the time Sean gets back to the house it's already late afternoon and he can hear the chunk and smack of dirt hitting the fence as he climbs out of the car. He heads straight for the side gate of his neighbor's house and reaches over to unlatch it, knowing that it's nearly identical to his own. As he rounds the end of the house he sees Charlie panting as he leans over the shovel. He's suddenly, irrevocably, and acutely aware of the man's age. He waits for Charlie to turn around and notice him, pausing with rustling plastic bags in hand. He waits, almost too long, standing at the corner of the house frozen. Sean is uncertain but curious and when Charlie finally does turn around, it isn't the violent acknowledgement Sean has half expected, but something simpler and more honest, as if the older man was waiting for him.

"Sean," he says, "what brings you by? Afraid the old man here has finally lost what's left of his marbles?"

Sean gives a little laugh –attempting to ignore the question. The air around them is laced with the earthy smell of sweat and dirt.

"All this work you're doing. Thought you might be hungry."

"Hey? What you got there?"

"Steaks, potatoes, corn."

"Bring any beer?"

"Of course."

"Give me a minute to get cleaned up."

Sean waits on the back patio as Charlie slips out of his shoes and disappears into the house. For the moment he's on his own, in the unfamiliarity of his neighbor's backyard, and he knows for a fact that if Sara were to crane her neck to the left and angle her eyes out the window she'd see him sitting at the patio table with the grocery bags in front of him.

Charlie returns wearing a fresh shirt and pauses momentarily at the side door to slip on a pair of battered loafers as he smirks at Sean.

"Sorry to leave you out here. Didn't even think to ask you in."

"No worries."

"Wife sent you over to find out just what the heck old Charlie's doing tearing up a perfectly good backyard, hey?"

Charlie sits as if drawn quickly downwards by an unseen force. As he combs his snowy hair with his fingers Sean can see the shiny pink of the man's scalp. Sean reaches into one of the bags and snaps two cans from their plastic rings. Charlie must be digging himself a pool.

"Not exactly," Charlie says, "it's a fallout shelter. Well. It will be by the time I'm done."

"You're kidding."

"Never know when the fit hits the shan."

Sean glances at the pit; the ragged edges could easily be the set for any of the bad horror movies of Sean's misspent youth. Surely the guy has to be kidding. But if he's cracked he might actually be dangerous.

All those people that shoot up grocery stores and malls – they're like Charlie, aren't they? It's always the ones you don't suspect, or so they say, and for a moment Sean is worried. As he watches Charlie heave himself up from the chair he realizes how silly he's being. The guy has to be pushing seventy and it isn't as though he's fit for his age. He's your run-of-the-mill, skinny, old man that lives alone. Charlie makes his way over to the barbecue parked beneath the eave of the house and rolls it several feet away from the side of the house and reaches down to open the valve on the propane tank.

"We'll get this thing fired up and let her get up to temperature. Take it your wife isn't coming along."

"Had some things to do."

There's a stuttering click as Charlie holds down the button for the electric igniter and then the whoosh of the flame when it finally catches.

"You think old Charlie's cracked."

"Cracked?"

"Nuts. Bonkers. Certifiable. Padded Cells. The whole shebang."

"Nah."

"It's understandable," Charlie says, "Heck. You'd be nuts if you didn't think I was nuts, and it's fine. Really. I like the company, and it might just be your lucky day."

"Come again?"

Charlie sets his beer on the patio table and gestures for Sean to follow, and makes his way to the sliding door, kicking off his shoes as he steps inside. Sean reaches down to unlace his shoes, thinking maybe this is how the guy lures people into his dungeon. At a half-head taller and with a good twenty or thirty pounds on the guy, Sean reminds himself there's no need worry. After all, Sara knows where he is. Inside the house is dim and there is a vague musty smell that mingles with this morning's coffee and fried eggs. The carpet has been worn down, and Sean can see where the man has treaded, shuffling, perhaps in half-sleep from living room to kitchen and then down the hall to where the master bedroom must be.

Part way down the hall Charlie stops and turns gesturing through the open doorway. Inside the room Sean can see that two computers have been set up – or maybe one computer with two screens. On the wall an oversized map of the county is bordered by various newspaper articles pinned in a loose column. Sean nods, taking it all in. The blinds on the window are closed to slits, and other than the map and the articles the walls are bare.

"This is command central," Charlie says, "which's a figure of speech, by the way, it's not actually command anything. Just where I work. Look. You know what algorithms are? Type of thing they use on Google, all the Internet search engines. I worked with things like that the last few years of the career. Turns out it isn't too difficult to set one up to do a little searching of its own. Set the right parameters; let the thing run itself."

Charlie leads the way into the room and sits down in the rolling chair and taps the keyboard, the displays come to life, an intricate matrix of maps and headlines.

"I guess this isn't helping any. You came out here to find out I'm not a nutcase, and this only proves it, right?"

"Are you, Charlie?"

"He asks the question. Good for you. Has Charlie lost his marbles? Well, maybe."

"Maybe?"

"Would I know if I had?"

Despite himself Sean feels a smile crease his face but he's uncertain what to say, as if any comment might spark the dry tinder of Charlie's precarious paranoia. How's he to know that the wrong word or phrase might cause Charlie to snap and pull a gun from the desk drawer.

Although his beer is empty he holds onto it, because it's something to do. Something to occupy himself with. Eventually it might be an excuse to get out of the room. Charlie presses a key and the screens go black as he rolls back his chair and stands up, leading the way back through the dining room to the sliding door. He's thankful to be outside again, in the still warm air. The cross breeze prickles the skin at the back of his neck. There's a fine rope of smoke coming from the lid of the barbecue, and they can smell the charcoal layer burning off of the grill. The men stand there watching the flames tickle the metal grate and Sean retrieves two more beers from the bag, forgetting that Charlie has left a barely touched beer on the patio table. Charlie ducks back inside for tinfoil and a plate and utensils to start the potatoes going. Saying they'll need a while to get going. Once they have rolled the potatoes in foil and set them on the grill the two men stand in a prolonged silence.

"Come on," Charlie says finally, "I'll show you the other part of this whole deal."

Sean's worry is melting into curiosity as he follows Charlie around the side of the house to the garage. Inside he can see that there is no longer room for Charlie to park his old pickup, which sits leaking its daily dose of oil onto the driveway. Charlie has lined the walls of the garage with metal shelves and there are two large folding tables set up in the middle of the room. Sean can see without asking that the shelves are laden with enough canned food to stock a corner store. There are large jugs of water and what looks to be fifty-gallon drum of fuel.

"This is only part," Charlie says, "I have to keep the rest of it a secret. Never know. The fit hits the shan and you might be knocking on my door for help. Or, you might be knocking on my door to take what I've got."

"I don't think I'd do that."

"Exactly. You don't think you would, but desperate times desperate measures."

"You expecting some sort of apocalypse?"

"Weren't you ever a Boy Scout?"

Sean shakes his head and imagines circular merit badge emblazoned with a fiery mushroom cloud. Charlie makes a gesture and leads them back out into the driveway before pulling the door down and waiting for it to click. They walk back around the side of the house and now, finally, Charlie's beer is empty and he reaches into the bag and grabs another for himself. They return to their seats at the patio table. The smell of the barbecue and the late Spring evening and the beer are putting Sean in a decent mood. He hasn't spent an afternoon like this in longer than he can remember. Sean and Sara's friends are all well-intentioned but they seem to spend more time concerned about construction on I-5 or housing prices to ever worry about something like this.

"Ask you a question?" Charlie says after a long pull on his beer.

"Shoot."

"You have car insurance."

"Sure."

"Fire. Earthquake. Life? Same thing."

Charlie explains that after Margaret left he had more time to spend looking into these things. Sure it had been part of what had made her leave. All those years of marriage and it just went out the window because she thought that he had finally lost it and she couldn't stand to be in the house with him anymore. She was worried that he was going to completely lose his mind, and the arguments had tunneled beneath the once sturdy walls of their relationship and when it was thoroughly compromised the whole thing collapsed.

The whole time that the relationship was eroding Charlie was monitoring the news: an outbreak of West Nile in Florida. Civil War in the Congo. Flesh eating bacteria in a New York hospital. Then there were the historical events. The San Francisco Earthquake of 1989. Hurricane Sandy. Hurricane Katrina. Chernobyl. Fukushima.

Even if it wasn't a nuclear holocaust that ended the world as we know it, he wanted to be able to survive. He's old, he knows that, but that doesn't mean that he has to resign himself to death. The two men sip their beers and Charlie finally gets up to put the steaks on the barbecue, tearing into the plastic package with his fingernail.

By the time they finally pull the steaks off of the barbecue the sun has set in brilliant oranges and pinks and the sky is drifting steadily towards the muddy blue- gray of night. By now Sean has a good solid buzz going, and he knows Charlie has been matching him one-for-one since they started, and he has to admit that the older man seems in good spirits; he's becoming even more talkative. Their silverware catches the glint of the back porch lights and the steaks practically sparkle.

"Tell you the truth," Sean says as he finishes his steak, "you do seem a little bit nutty."

"There you go. Good man. Honesty."

"Nutty but maybe a little realistic. I don't know if that makes sense."

"I get it," he says, "Trust me. If anyone you know is bound to understand that it's me."

"What did you expect your neighbors to think?"

Charlie looks at him in the half-light and smiles, shrugs, "life insurance."

"And your pit here?"

"That there is the platinum membership."

Sean pulls himself up from his seat and walks to the edge of the ragged hole. The sod is frayed and uneven at the end, and he can see the larger rocks where he has begun to pile them in the center.

"You have some sort of blueprint, I imagine."

"Designed it myself."

"Looks like this project's going to take you a while."

"If fit hits the shan before I can get her done, so be it."

"I meant alone."

"He's coming around, folks."

It's just after midnight when Sara rolls over in bed and realizes that Sean isn't home yet. She glances at the glowing red numbers of the alarm clock and momentary panic stalks through her veins. Throwing back the covers she slips on her robe and pads softly down the hallway to the kitchen, pausing there scrutinizing the silence until something, instinct maybe, leads her to the kitchen window. On tiptoes she cranes her neck again, just as she had that morning, peering over the fence into Charlie's backyard.

    It's so incongruous that it takes her a moment to recognize her husband's body as the muscles of his back move like hinges in sweat gleaming moonlight as he digs a shovel into the earth and flings earth towards the fence. Nearby, standing knee-deep in the pit beside her husband is Charlie, alternating movements with Sean. A strange choreography of pick and shovel. She hasn't heard the noise – but now she can hear it through the window – the distant chunk swish of the shovel. Sarah leans over the sink and begins to cry.

Evidence of Life

It happens like this: after a night of drinking he pisses on the hood of a parked police car. It's one of those days. He's been fired from his job as a short-order cook for mouthing off to his boss again. Two hours of double rum and cokes later he is stumbling home with an over-full bladder.

"You seeing this?" a voice behind him asks.

The two cops wait for James to finish. They watch with crossed arms, hiding smirks.

"Shake it more than twice," one says, "and you're playing with it."

He barely gets himself put away before he's stumbling backwards falling over a sapling planted along the curb. Vice-like hands clutch his biceps. He feels the grip through his rum-addled thoughts. He's barely found the ground when he's hustled into the back of the police car. They process him at county lockup. Fluorescent lights on beige cinderblocks amplify the worst hangover he's ever had. At twenty-three he's never been in trouble like this before. Yet, even the cops don't take his crime seriously. In the other room he can hear them laughing. After sitting on a cold cement bench for hours he finds himself in front of a judge. James' hands are cuffed in front of him. His wrists are raw, and his shoulders ache from having to keep his hands clasped in front of him.

"Come on, it was harmless," James says.

The judge is an indifferent, heavy-set man in a black robe.

"Public indecency. Public drunkenness. Destruction of public property."

"Victimless."

The judge hands down his sentence: a five hundred dollar fine and forty hours of community service. Without any money left in his pockets James starts the slow walk home. It takes him a little more than an hour, down exhausted streets. By the time he gets home it's early afternoon, but he has nothing to stay awake for. He has no job, no way to pay the fine, and no idea how to get through the next couple of weeks. There's beer left in the refrigerator and spaghetti congealing on plates beside the sink.

The alcohol makes its way through his system and momentarily quiets his thoughts. For a time – somewhere between the end of the third beer and the beginning of the fifth – his thoughts quiet. When the beer takes over his system completely the room circles, mercilessly. He sleeps long enough for the drumming pulse against his temples to fade away, and wakes more sober. It's early evening, the sun is at a depressing angle – not low enough to be considered night, not high enough to be considered day.

The easiest way to serve his community service is road duty, picking up trash along the freeway. Five days of community service. Standing in his boxers he counts the spare change on the dresser beside his bed. Between the loose change and the crumpled bills, he has a little more than twenty dollars. There'll be another paycheck on Friday; his last check from his old job, and it won't be much. James pulls on his jeans and walks aimlessly from the kitchen to the bedroom to the living room and back. It's not pacing so much as sleepwalking through the same rooms over and over again.

James is nursing a beer on the couch when his roommate, David, gets home from an equally depressing day at the grocery store on the corner. As James gazes through the TV he hears the refrigerator door open and close behind him, and then he can tell that David is standing behind him. David smells of fish and rotting produce, and doesn't bother to change before sitting down on the couch. The beer can hisses as he opens it, the thin metal crinkling in his hand.

"Community service?"
"It's bullshit."
"Community fucking service."
"Tell me about it."

David rests the can on his knee and picks something from his lower lip, a stray bit of skin or tobacco.

"Pissing on a cop car."
"When you gotta go."

After making their way through the rest of the beer they both pass out – James on his bed, and David on the couch. Empty cans and dirty plates crowd the kitchen counter. In the middle of the night stray and antagonistic thoughts hold reality and practicality at a distance. His breath is weighted down by cinder blocks.

It takes the bus nearly an hour to get from his apartment to the police station. Mash transit. The bus stinks of urine in afternoon heat. He doesn't have a car or a license and doesn't know anyone who can give him a ride. David's passed out on the couch, and his rusting Honda is still sitting by the curb on 51st. James admits to himself that the Honda wouldn't have been much better.

He's early to rollcall. A big white van with metal grates over the windows sits near the precinct entrance. Two men in khaki pants and dark green polo shirts stand near the van shooting the shit and sipping coffee from paper cups. As James walks over to the men they look up at him, the older of the two is a solid looking guy with steely hair, who introduces himself as Sergeant Prosser. Prosser is the man in charge, and might have been a pit-bull in a previous life. The other guy is thinner and younger, with sandy blond hair and pitted skin.

"Have a seat," Prosser gestures absently to the curb with his clipboard.

Sitting on the low curb James peals a stray bit of rubber from the edge of his tennis shoe. The skies are gray and look like rain; in the meantime it's just damn gloomy. The thread of rubber comes free from his shoe and he rubs it into a ball between his thumb and index finger before dropping it onto the asphalt. A handful of cars pass on the street that borders the parking lot. A few of the cars pull into the parking lot and a small group of people wearily approach Prosser and check-in. By eight thirty there are seven smoking and impatient folks waiting to get the day over with.

"Take a vest and gloves and get in the van," Prosser says.

Sanderson hands out the vests and gloves as Prosser ticks names off on his clipboard. The seven of them cram into the van with their vests and gloves in their laps. Dimly, James is aware of the coarse mesh of the bright orange vest and the gumminess of the latex gloves. From the corner of his eye James looks around the van. Prosser climbs into the driver's seat and Sanderson rides shotgun. As he adjusts down into his seat Prosser plugs the keys into the ignition and puts his sunglasses on before turning around.

"Stay off the road. Don't cross onto the freeway. Don't pick up anything dangerous. Razor blades, needles, shards of metal. You will not pick these things up."

James sets down the garbage bag and pulls at his gloves, tugging them farther down over his wrists. The light blue latex stretches over the backs of his hands; there's a prickly feeling on his skin from the trapped sweat. The closer he looks into the long bristles of grass the more bits and pieces of trash he sees. Bottles cans and paper seem to unearth themselves – seem to grow up out of the embankment like weeds. There is some semblance of progress. Part of a bumper lies in the ditch, a "Honk if you love

Jesus" sticker curling away from the plastic. The leavings of other people's lives.

They stack the orange plastic bags, stuffed full of garbage, into lumpy pyramids beside the road for another crew to come along and pick up. He considers the fact that people have left trash beside the road, and he has done little more than gather it up for another crew to come pick up, and there will be another crew after that and another. The garbage slowly migrating towards some landfill where it will simply sit, relocated, and passive.

After four hours they are loaded back into the van, which Prosser calls "The Bus," and are driven back to the precinct. James feels a dim sensation that no time has really passed at all – although there are more cars in the parking lot and there are more cars passing along the street on the far side of the parking lot. Sanderson collects the bright orange vests as Prosser checks their names off of a clipboard. As he waits to turn in his vest he looks around at the other workers, most of them don't seem interested in making eye contact. There's a girl at the end of the line that's horsing around with a burly, construction worker type.

"Life on the chain-gang," James says as he passes them.

"Another day another dollar," says the girl.

"We're headed out for a beer," says the construction worker.

"Where at?"

"Anywhere nearby."

"I know a place, can one of you give me a ride home afterwards?"

"How far?"

"Wallingford," James says, "I'll buy the first round."

The bar is a dim place that James has been to countless times before. It's not too far from his apartment, maybe a mile or two, an Irish place with big screen TV's and dark stained oak tables. Guinness posters and Gaelic road signs are tacked to the ceiling, and there are a handful of people sitting at the bar. It's a little after one in the afternoon. It wasn't too far to ride in Saul's pickup – the construction worker is much older than James originally thought. In the rattling old truck, he noticed silver at his temples and the cracked and calloused hands of a man used to hard labor. The three of them get a pitcher of beer and claim a booth at the far side of the room.

"What'd you do, anyways, bud?"

"Pissed on a cop car."

"You hate cops?"

"Not at all."

Saul and the girl, her name's Aubrey, laugh.

"Let me get this straight," Aubrey says, "you're walking along and you whip it out and let loose on the side of a cop car?"

"Not the side," he says, "the hood."

"Now that's something they don't expect to catch on dash-cams."

"You're telling me."

The three of them make their way through a few pitchers of beer. James is pretty quick to realize that the girl, Aubrey, has the hots for Saul. He can't quite figure out why. She's maybe twenty-one – at least half Saul's age and Saul is married with two teenage kids of his own. Turns out that none of them have done anything too serious, just barely serious enough to warrant a little community service. Aubrey had petty theft; Saul had a second drunk driving charge.

"Real hardened criminals, we are," Saul says and tips the last of the pitcher into Aubrey's glass. He gets up and walks to the bar for another pitcher. James looks over his shoulder watching the muscles stretching and contracting under Saul's thin sweatshirt; James turns back around and examines the grooves and divots in the table. He's trying to think of something to say to Aubrey, wanting to know more about her but not knowing what to ask.

"Got a girl?" she asks him. Her legs crossed, foot jiggling.

"Nope. You," he says, "I mean, you got a man?"

"Neither," she says. "You know how it is."

"What'd you steal?"

"Something I didn't need. Wasn't the first, won't be the last."

It's not long before Saul returns with another pitcher tops up their glasses, starting with Aubrey and ending with himself.

"I gotta get going after this one," Saul says.

"I should probably head out, too," James agrees, feeling the buzz of alcohol and the comfort of new acquaintances. Although Saul offers to drive him home James says he won't mind walking and it's not very far anyways. He wants some time to think, and is tired of talking. Spending money at the bar has reminded him how little cash he has left, and that he's got three more days before he can get his last paycheck from the restaurant.

"Don't piss on anything on your way home," Saul says shaking James' hand.

"Keep it in your pants, stud-muffin," Aubrey says.

The air is cool but the walk helps clear his head a bit. When he returns to the apartment he lays his wallet and keys on the dresser and lies down, falling asleep with his clothes on. At three AM he wakes up and walks out into the living room. The TV is on and David is passed out on the couch. James walks over and stares out the window, looking down at the street below their apartment before clicking the TV off and heading back to bed.

There's not much room for sleep for James between three AM and six AM when he has to get up to catch the bus back to the precinct for his second day of community service. He coaxes himself up out of bed at six and showers and dresses and catches the bus down to the precinct. After paying bus fair and buying a pitcher of beer the night before he has $10.18 left.

The squeal and ratcheting of the door cracks at his temples as the bus eases up along the curb. The wind, abrasive, pushes against the side of his face and lifts his hair into impatient threads.   Prosser is waiting beside the van with Sanderson. The two men are dressed the same in their khakis and green polos and have on dark brown jackets. They are standing on the lee side of the van, a little out of the wind, although the residual air that cuts over the top of the van lifts and drops the papers on Prosser's clipboard.

"Welcome to day two," says Sanderson.

James nods sits down against the rear tire of the van and tries to shrink down into his sweatshirt, pulling the hood up over his head and clamping his hands between his knees. Beneath him the cold concrete isn't helping matters.

Third to show up, after a gaunt looking guy that could be Hispanic or Arabic or Indian, is Aubrey. She sits down beside James and lays her head on his shoulder.

"Damn it's cold."

"Windy."

"That too."

"Today's going to be a blast."

The pressure and warmth of her cheek is unfamiliar but comfortable. Ten minutes later Saul shows up and walks over and stands in front of them in his faded Carhartt jacket and a black watch cap. Splatters of paint and plaster cling to Saul's shoes. The drill is the same: clipboard, vest, into the van. Other than Prosser and Sanderson there are only six of them in the van. After fifteen minutes of driving Prosser eases the van off onto the shoulder of I-5 near the Shoreline exit, cranks the E-break back and cuts the engine.

"All right, same old same old," he says. "Be careful."

They pile out of the bus and James pulls his hoodie up over his head and tugs on the plastic gloves. The three of them – James, Saul and Aubrey – wander south along the northbound lane, walking on the uneven embankment. The dirt is damp and sinks under their feet. Cars displace the air on the freeway and send concussion waves up the embankment, rattling the plastic of the garbage bags and rippling their clothes.

To be on the freeway but not moving makes him feel vulnerable; the absence of insulation from the noise and cold makes him self-conscious. Ahead of him, Saul seems unaffected by the chill or the situation. James wishes that he were taller and broader, wishing that he took up more physical space – that he was more substantial. Instead he bends, stoops, picks up a wax lined cup and its plastic lid. A dribble of gritty water drains onto the grass.

Another four hours passes the same as the day before, but this time, he doesn't go out afterwards. Too tired and too broke. The wind and the grayness of the sky have made him irritable, and all he wants to do is go home and shower. He can smell the exhaust and the cold and the dirt on his clothes.

Three more days of road crew. Two more days until he can pick up his check. Nine dollars left in his pocket and six beers left in the fridge. In the early evening there is only the barest amount of light that sifts through the curtains, rendering his bedroom in black and white. He pulls the covers tighter around himself; the cold crawls along his shoulders and down his spine to the small of his back. He fantasizes about a perfect crime, something that would set him up for the rest of his life – like a heist in an old gangster movie. Pinstripe suits and cockeyed hats. Or, better, an imperfect crime. One in which no one gets hurt and he gets caught. The need for money and decisions ceases in that potential capture – a slow slipping of time and life in an anonymous cell.

The third day of road crew is uneventful and the need for money is more pressing than ever. He's picked over almost everything in the kitchen, eating stale crackers and scraping the dredges of peanut butter from the jar with a spoon.

There must be a solution, he thinks, something that will solve his problems. At eight in the evening, he pries himself out of bed and pulls on his jeans and his hoodie, starts the walk over to the restaurant, still trying to decide if he'll simply ask for his check or if he'll ask for his job back. Beg for his job back. He hates the idea. The boss is an asshole, and the last thing that he wants to do is apologize to the guy, but there seem to be few other options.

The restaurant is mellow that late at night, an hour to closing time, and he makes his way to the bar and sits down in one of the padded chairs. From the far end of the bar he catches the bartender's eye. The man shakes his head slowly without smiling as he walks towards James.

"I don't know," the bartender says.
"I'm just here for my check."
"They aren't here until tomorrow."
"I was hoping."
"I'll see."

The bartender folds a towel into a neat rectangle and lays it on the counter behind the bar, and heads off in search of someone to talk to James. Counting until thirty, James takes a deep breath and glances over his shoulder. The evening manager is a woman that he never had any problem with, she was about the same age as James, but more of a college type who seemed to dress ten years older than she actually was, as if she were only playing the character of a manager in a school play. James can't remember her name but smiles at her all the same, as she approaches him from behind the bar.

"No checks yet, James," she says.
"I was also wondering."

"They're not going to give you your job back, James."

"I'm in a tough spot."

"I can understand that," she says, "but they won't do it."

James heaves himself up from the bar stool and thanks her as coolly as he can. Although the restaurant is close to the apartment it never seemed closer; James needs some time to clear his head and the walk isn't quite long enough to do it. He continues past the apartment, weaving around buildings until he eventually finds himself back at the apartment, ever conscious of how close he is. Conscious of the lack of money and all that it means.

The apartment isn't empty and James is having a hard time deciding on whether or not that's a good thing or a bad thing. David is sitting on the couch watching TV, his apron tossed onto the battered coffee table, two empty beer cans crumpled but standing upright in little puddles of condensation.

"Beer and pizza."

"Thank God."

"Thank Payday."

James cracks a beer and sits down on the couch.

"How much time do you have left?"

"Two more days."

"And then?"

"I find a new job," James says. "I get my last paycheck tomorrow."

David leans back against the couch and stares at the ceiling. Two of his knuckles are cracked and bleeding, the skin peeled back in little threads. James examines his own hands, there's a broad burn scar across the back of his hand that is just starting to heal. He picks at the scab, scratching the irritated red edges of the wound with his thumbnail.

"We might need another stocker at work," David says without shifting his gaze from the ceiling.

"I don't know if I could go back there."

They'd met at the grocery store several years back, when James was still in culinary school. James called it a marriage of convenience – rooming together to ease up the cost of living. James hadn't been fired from the store, but he had quit amid a loud argument with a customer. As he thinks about it he's angry at himself for dropping out of culinary school.

He has no idea what to do for work; the restaurant is no longer an option, and he knows that now. He thinks briefly of Saul and the construction business but he knows that it isn't something that he could do – he can't picture it in his head, and that's usually the standard that he judges options by. If he can't imagine it then it must not be worth doing.

His thoughts return to the crime, but added is the fantasy of ending it all. But he isn't the suicidal type and never was. First, it would be next to impossible to decide what method to use. And the note. And the thought of his parents thinking of him, dead, having committed suicide is even worse than the act itself – the ends outweigh the means. There is no way that he can get a job and pay rent by the end of the month.

He leaves his room only for another beer. Long after David is passed out James goes on drinking, until the point that he knows that he'll still be drunk when he shows up for roadcrew. He knows that he'll sober up somewhere along I-5 in the chill of the afternoon and the concussion of the passing cars. But he wants none of it now. He wants to live in the present for whatever the present is worth – which he is sure is very, very little.

After cashing his last check, and one last half-hearted attempt at trying to get his job back he finds himself at the last day of road crew. Aubrey is smiles and Saul seems in about the same mood. James wishes that he felt the same – that there was something to indicate to him that it was all over, but he has larger concerns now, like how to pay his bills. It was what got him into this mess in the first place, after all. The need for money, the loss of job. He hasn't bothered to look for a new job and has no excuse now.

The day is as dull as any other. He fantasizes about finding a winning lotto ticket, a bag of cash, anything, something that would take his mind off of his problems – not only, but something that would take his mind off of his problems, but something that would solve his problems. Just as jumping in front of a semi rushing at 70 miles per hour down I-5 would solve his problems. But he can't bring himself to do it. For better or worse he is married to the idea of life.

"Wake up," Aubrey says.

"I'm good."

"You're in fucking lala land."

"It's nothing."

"Don't tell me you're going to miss this shit."

"That's exactly it," he says, "I was trying to figure out how I could spend the rest of my life in this shit-storm that they call community service."

The slow afternoon traffic backs up across four lanes of southbound I-5. Brake lights and glossy cars in all different sorts of condition idle so near by that in some cases James can hear the music buzzing and thumping out of windows, rattling license plates. It's a raw sort of tedium, but James is as anonymous as anyone who might be stuck by the side of the road. At least as anonymous as anything that didn't require flashing lights.

This is how it has always been for him: he is only a bystander. The thought should worry him, or at least make him think about his lot in life. He knows that, but it no longer bothers him. He is here and the cars are here and the trash is here waiting to be scooped into the bright orange trash bags. There's a morbid hope that there will be some accident or some gruesome fault that will bring excitement to the day, but there is nothing, only the daily frustration of people stuck in cars cursing construction or a suspected accident that has clogged the lanes.

When the day is over and Prosser orders them all back onto the bus, James sits down next to Aubrey, who smiles at him – a distracted sort of smile. Again he wishes that there was something to say, something that he knew should be said, but life isn't a movie and he is stuck with half-formed thought and un-utterable phrases.

"That's it," Aubrey says.

"End of story," he says without looking over at her.

"Fat lady has sung."

"Is that what was holding up traffic?" Saul says from a seat behind them.

The idea of it makes James smirk: a fat woman standing in the middle of the freeway, sequined gown and high eyebrows. Her voice lifting towards the overpass and bouncing back. Not so much an echo as a fading a ripple of sound, devoid of the richness that had once been there. And he thinks: this is the simplicity of it all.

And here's how it ends: Prosser checks them out as if it were any other day. In fact, the old bastard probably doesn't even give a shit that it's the last day of community service for most of them. There's no sense of responsibility, that he's done his part to get his road crew through the experience without injury. He's done his job to help rehabilitate minor offenders. None of that. The guy could scarcely give a gigantic flying fuck. But here they all are in the parking lot staring at the fan and watching Prosser and Sanderson pack the dayglow orange vests into a duffle bag and lock up and head inside the precinct with their clipboards and dark brown jackets.

"Beer?" Aubrey nudges his shoulder.

"I'm pretty broke, Aubrey."

"It's a celebration," she says, "you deserve a few."

"It's what got me into this in the first place."

"Hey," Saul says." Pull yourself together, sad sack, it's just a beer to celebrate the fact that we're done with this community service bullshit. At least until next time."

James imagines the fat lady again, her hair swept back over her shoulder, the honking cars and angry drivers pounding their steering wheels, hurling obscenities. The woman is in mid-aria with her eyes closed and she notices nothing.

Second Run

"They see only their own shadows, or the shadows of one another, which the fire throws on the opposite wall..."
   --Plato, Allegory of the Cave

The empty lot used to be a supermarket until it was torn down. Weeds and dying grass stitch together the broken concrete. Cans, cigarette butts, and crumpled fast food wrappers drift across the asphalt. Laura ducks through the gap in the chain link fence at the far end of the lot, where the metal has been peeled away from the posts. The reader board above the Valley Movie Theater is a dingy yellow wedge pointed at the highway. The mismatched letters are a collection of black and red, numbers stand in for both capital and lower case letters.

Laura pulls her baggy jacket around her as she enters the stale popcorn smell of the lobby. The intermittent sounds of the video games lined up along the far wall bang and rattle. She ignores the vaulted ceilings and stares the duct-tape patched carpeting.

In the small break room Laura takes off her jacket and puts on the red bow tie and satiny black vest she's required to wear. The daily assignments are listed on a clipboard hanging from the wall. She stares at the list and tries to focus on the names. This is her seventh shift in as many days, and she has had a hard time sleeping, the evening shifts throwing her schedule out of whack. Laura's daily assignment, along with Chance, is: "Guest Comfort".

She pushes through the heavy metal door and emerges into the lobby. Manager Dave and Crystal are behind the concession's counter. Dave is explaining something about the soda machine. He dumps pitchers of ice into the top of the machine and checks the syrup levels. Crystal is newish, a high school kid. Laura has yet to have a conversation with her, but they've been introduced several times.

When a movie lets out Laura and Chance stands in the hallway making sure no one screen surfs from one movie to another. A movie is letting out, and several families make their way towards the lobby – small kids sprint down the hallway. Smaller kids are carried by their parents. Here in the lobby the lighting prevents shadows. During the summer, it isn't until you exit the building that the sun stings your eyes; the overwhelming brightness.

Laura and Chance stand aside and let the families pass. When the next film begins they stand at the entrance to the long hallway and collect tickets, dropping them one at a time into the podium situated between scarlet ropes. Once the film starts they walk through the theater and to make sure people are reasonably well behaved. After the movies end they walk through the cavernous screening rooms and pick up Abba-Zabba and Butterfinger wrappers. They sweep stray popcorn from the sticky floors.

Rain scatters against the front windows. It promises to be a slow night, which is good. Laura will be able to slip into one of the movies and watch, or, more likely, fall asleep curled in one of the chairs in the back row. She never has much trouble sleeping here. There is comfort sleeping in a large room as a movie plays. The soundtracks and dialogue invade her dreams.

A young couple comes in and heads into a movie that has already started. They're ten minutes late, but they don't seem to be in a hurry. They are high school kids, probably seniors. Crystal nods to them and smiles in a way that says she knows them – a dim familiarity. Chance walks over to where Laura is running the vacuum back and forth over the same patch of carpet.

"We could mess with them," he says.

"We could," she says.

Chance shrugs and walks away. Laura vacuums the threadbare carpet. When she is done with one patch she puts the vacuum away and checks the ladies' room. She scoops a handful of crumpled paper towels off the counter and tosses them in the garbage. The arcade games along the wall make roaring spaceship noises and the sounds of explosions and gunfire.

The rain comes down in sheets, creating broad lakes of water in the low areas of the parking lot. A group of teenagers comes in. Four in all, moving like puppies, clumping together, tripping over one another.

They yap and bark at each other. They shake their coats and throw back their hoods – the shoulders of their jackets stained dark with rain, and hair dripping across their foreheads. They split into groups, the girls head to the concessions counter and the boys head towards the video games. Chance straightens up and walks around the concessions counter to help Crystal with the orders of popcorn, extra-large sodas, Jujubes, Junior Mints.

Laura positions herself behind the podium between the ropes. On the top are numbered slots – each slot represents a screen. The kids bound up with popcorn and sodas and candy.

"Screen Four, down the hall on the left," she says tearing the tickets.

"Screen Four," she says, "Screen Four."

She hands the tickets back and drops the stubs into the slot for Screen Four. Chance heads back to start the movie, and Laura goes past the other screen to check on the couple in Screen Two, whose movie will be ending soon. The couple is sitting in the middle row in the middle of the theater. The girl's head leans on the guy's shoulder and his head is leans over on top of hers. The way people stare straight forward at the screen for hours at a time is always strange to her.

Laura watches the screen a moment before slipping out and down Screen Four. The kids have the theater to themselves. They jump over the seats and throw popcorn at each other. The two boys are up near the projector window creating shadow puppets on the screen. Laura is beyond caring whether or not they mess up the theater. In the hallway she runs into Chance. He asks if the kids in Screen Four are behaving.

"Like kids," she says.

"Did you talk to them?"

Laura shrugs. The wind buffets against the lobby windows. She stands staring at the windows. David asks if she's already checked the bathrooms.

"Take your fifteen," he says, "send Chance when you get back."

Laura grabs an extra-large soda from concessions, hoping the caffeine will keep her awake. The syrup coats her teeth in sugary fuzz as she sits otherwise motionless at the break table. The sugar sits like a ball in the pit of her stomach. She feels tired and slightly sick from the soda. She walks through the lobby and nods to Chance and Chance nods back and heads to the break room for his fifteen. In Screen Four the kids have mostly settled down and are intermittently shouting at the screen.

She continues to vacuum, not because the carpet is dirty, but because she has nothing else to do. She vacuums down the hall, edging in overlapping angles. One of the boys from theater four comes out, full of a smiling, predatory energy. His age is hard to discern. He watches Laura like he has the perfect joke. Laura looks up at him as he pulls a crumpled pack of Marlboros from his jacket pocket.

"Smoke?"

"I just took a break."

"You look busy."

Laura glances up as Chance comes out of the break room. He slips his cell phone into his pocket and walks over to where Crystal is leaning on the counter, no doubt leaving greasy arm prints on the glass. She figures that David much be in the office. Laura slips into the break room for her jacket and walks outside with the boy.

In the alley behind the theater, near the dumpsters, he puts his back to the wind and lights his cigarette, then shields the flame for her. She has to lean close-ish to him, and she can see the black crescents of his fingernails as the flame wavers. They stand exposed to the wind and rain, trying to use the dumpster as a windbreak. Smoke drifts up and away from them in stages – blowing first one way and then another – sometimes just hanging low beside them like some sea creature caught in the wavering undercurrents of the wind. Shadows of trees waver on the wall above and behind them. He drops his cigarette and chases it with his foot, dragging a toe across the cigarette as it rolls away. Sparks scatter into momentary constellations.

Laura shivers and takes a long last draw on her cigarette. The kid skips and hops next to her as they enter through the front door of the theater. Chance looks up at her curiously and Crystal smiles with a knowingly. Crystal's smile is the secretive sort that seems beyond her high school years. Laura hangs up her jacket in the break room; the cold dampness of the jacket in her hands.

She refills her soda, the straw squeaking as she stabs it through the lid. The taste of wax and sugar and cloying syrup. It's barely keeping her awake. The young couple that was alone in screen two walks out arm in arm, and Chance walks down the hall to clean the theater. Even though there were only two people in Screen Two Chance will walk down both aisles and check most of the seats, sweep the floor. For the most part it is another way to take up time; to inch ever closer to the end of the shift.

Shortly after the couple leaves Dave sends Chance home. Chance jogs across the parking lot to his car. Laura watches as the headlights come on, and the wipers bounce across the windshield. A low cloud of exhaust builds turning red in the brake lights before Chance tears across the parking lot and out onto the highway.

There is only one more late night showing, the 12:10. And the three of them: Dave, Crystal, and Laura will be enough to close up. They'll shut down Screens Three, Four, and Five and it will be even easier to close. They have to stay through the first half of the film before they can shut down if no one comes in.

Screen Four lets out. The kids come out into the hallway, slightly more subdued then when they went in. Two of the girls are walking arm in arm, weaving against each other. It's obvious that they've been drinking. It's not unusual. In fact, it's such a common thing; they almost assume that it's going to happen.

Passing into the lobby The Kid stays behind. He digs into his pocket and pulls out a handful of quarters. Standing before the shooting game, feet at shoulder width, he begins pumping quarters in. He takes it seriously, eyes locked on the screen. There is intensity to the way that he shoots. Focused and determined. He lines up quarters on the ledge of the game so that he can pump them in one after another. When he runs low he jogs over to concessions and cashes in several crumpled dollars for quarters.

Dave comes back down the hallway having locked up all the screens except Screen One. The film is cued up and the cinema is reasonably clean. Dave sends Laura to gather up the garbage. She takes the rolling trash bin from the cleaning closet and pushes it down the long hallway to Screen Five. After emptying the trashcans beside the entrance to each screen Laura trundles the cart outside. She shivers as she heaves the cart over the ruts and cracks of the uneven parking lot.

Laura realizes that what she thought was rain is only water flying off of the trees in the parking lot. Bright colored leaves plaster themselves to the cement – bright oranges, yellows, rust reds. The colors only slightly muted by the damp. As she parks the gray bin at an angle next to the dumpster to keep it from rolling away she wishes she'd grabbed her jacket. The lights on the side of the building are a dim fluorescent glow. She hoists one bag onto the lip of the dumpster and nudges it. She listens to the heavy thudding of the bags as they hit the bottom. The hollow bass sound as echoes down the alley.

Cigarette butts cluster at the base of the dumpster. As she lets the dumpster lid drop back into place Laura wonders how old The Kid actually is. Above her, on the wall, the shadows are painted on the bricks. She wheels the bin back towards the front doors and through the lobby, but The Kid is gone.

There's a slow dissipation of minutes as they wait for the evening to end. Dave, Crystal and Laura lounge at the concessions counter, watching the clock, hoping that no one else will come in so that they can leave early. Laura thinks only of curling into her bed and cocooning herself in the blankets and pillows. Dave and Crystal are talking about new movies that they wish were playing at the theater. Dave has an encyclopedic knowledge of films.

"I wanted to be a director when I was a kid," he says.

"I think it would be cool to be in a movie," Crystal says.

"Sure, acting is one thing," he says, "but directing."

"If the movie flops it's always the actors."

"The audience only sees what the director wants."

Laura refills her soda yet again and replaces the lid. Dave checks his watch and says they might as well shut it down. He locks the front doors and turns off the sign. He pulls the tills from the ticket booth and Laura and Crystal set to work shutting down the concessions counter, wiping down the surfaces and restocking the candy. The cinema is quiet and chilly. At a quarter to one they are turning out the lights and gathering at the front door, while Dave sets the alarm and then lets them out into the parking lot. The rain shatters the smooth surface of the puddles. Crystal climbs into her boyfriend's pickup and Dave crosses to his sedan. They shout goodbyes to each other.

Laura walks around the end of the building and ducks under the fence and pulls her jacket tight around her. The heavy wind pushes against her thighs as it comes low across the parking lot, rattling empty wrappers and beer cans. She reaches the far end of the parking lot and glances over her shoulder at the empty lot. Inside her apartment she locks the door and crosses to the window and looks down at the street. In the early morning breeze there is nothing but shadows.

The Filled in Spaces

"Waking consciousness is dreaming – but dreaming constrained by external reality."
--Dr. Oliver Sacks.

For the third morning in a row Edna wakes from a dream that doesn't belong to her. She wakes stunned again by the sadness of the orphaned dream. Beside her Alan is sound asleep, oblivious to this thing that has grown unchecked and unbidden in her unconsciousness; this foreign thing that has supplanted the predictability of her own circadian rhythms.

She sits up in the grainy darkness of the bedroom, comforted by the geometric regularity of nightstand and dresser and recliner. She is comforted by the predictability of Alan's breathing; by the certainty that he is dreaming the same dreams that he has dreamed for years now. Understandably she is discomfited by the intrusion of this dream that she is certain does not belong to her. Even now the residue of a stolen dream is sticky pollen against her eyelids.

Her threadbare T-shirt adheres to her skin as she shifts her legs towards the edge of the bed, careful not to wake her husband. Reaching for the glass on her nightstand she finds less than a sliver of water visible in the dimness. She is parched. Dying for water.

Wakefulness and sleep begin to fuse like the two halves of a broken bone knitting themselves back together as she shuffles from bedroom to bathroom to kitchen to living room. She leaves a trail of cast off things in her wake. Half empty mugs of tea. A crust of bread on a torn paper towel. A shopping list for things that they haven't run out of yet.

In every dream that she's ever owned she has been able to recognize herself. When Alan asks her how she slept she says fine. She must be coming down with something. This is not a complete or intangible lie. She does feel as though there is a virus settling into her tendons. Her appetite wanes.

Alan picks up the thread of a former argument. An I-hate-to-say-I-told-you-so smugness slithers onto his face. Perhaps she has returned to work too soon after Liam left for college after all. Perhaps she should allow the empty nest to settle in around her.

"Emptiness?"

"Nest," he says, "empty nest."

Alan bends to tie his shoes, car keys jangling in his hand. He is standing by the front door, his briefcase perched beside him on the floor. She watches the swift, precise movement of left over right, left over right. When he is finished tying his shoes he lets out an almost inaudible groan as he straightens. Edna is not convinced that this is a true groan. Perhaps it is only a telegraph of what he thinks is old age now that he is the father of a college student.

Edna's reality is crippled and limping; the stranger's dream gnaws at the edges of her consciousness. The act of recall has become, in itself, an act of censure. She tells herself that this is only a matter of a dream that has escaped the fenced in confines of its owner's mind. She tells herself that the dream must be returned.

On the morning of the fifth day she sits in the kitchen as day slowly emerges from night. She fusses with the wording of a lost and found ad, penning and repenning, crossing out words and thumbing the tattered thesaurus that she's retrieved from the shelf above Alan's desk. Maybe, she tells herself, not all dreams are intimate and personal. Surely the majority of dreams are inane and incomprehensible even to the dreamer, making little to no sense. But own, in the haziness that exists between night and day she wonders if the dreams are out there, hanging in the air like radio waves, waiting for the right transceiver to pick up the sound. Waiting for the right conduit to pick up the frequency.

For the longest time Edna could barely remember her dreams, let alone comprehend them, but there is something in this dream that seems to make her believe that this dream bears the weight of importance to the dreamer. And, in the meantime, she can't help but wonder where her dreams have gone. Is there some strange chain reaction of misplaced dreams, dominoing one after another?

She walks the aisles of the dollar store, skimming her eyes over things that she would never buy. She can't remember having ever come into one of these stores before. She is dimly aware of a memory of her mother. Her mother would frown at these dollar stores as places for people too petty to spend the extra money on quality. She feels like someone else.

An overly helpful employee pauses beside her and she shakes her head no. No, she does not need any help just now, not the type of help that could be offered. Only if the employee were able to explain how and why such things happen. With increasing regularity, she wonders whose life it is that she is living and whether or not a true self stumbles down these aisles. Exhausted she shuffles through the dollar store and nearly collides with strangers, muttering incomprehensible apologies that tinkle like broken glass on the floor behind her.

Part way through the morning of the sixth day she wakes to Alan's hand on her shoulder. It's the odd warmth of his hand that dislodges her from sleep. The dream fractures, spider-webbing at the edges and finally imploding. At first the things in the dream begin to change, and then she realizes it's only the intrusion of a familiar voice that exists outside the dream itself.

"You're having a bad dream," he says.
"Oh."
"You were talking in your sleep."

"What was I saying?"

"Couldn't make it out. Not words, really. Sounds."

For a moment she wants to berate him. Interrogate him. What had he heard exactly? What could he tell her about the dream that she was having and who it might belong to? Why would he wake her from the first dream that she can ever remember having in color?

The woman who answers the ad is not what Edna would have expected. She has a lupine face – all angles that seem pulled sharply towards the tip of her nose. The sharpness is intensified by the tight sweep of her ponytail, so precise that Edna can see the crisp rows that the brush has raked through her hair. She is easily twenty years younger than Edna.

"Sometimes it seems as though we go about carefully engineering gaps in our own lives," the woman says.

"Dreams aren't necessarily gaps," Edna says, "they're filled in spaces."

"Are we speaking metaphorically?"

"It's always hard to tell when we talk about dreams."

The woman picks at the edge of the Formica table, where the narrow bordering strip has come loose. As she lets go of the edge it's like a ruler vibrating against a tabletop, the pitch sliding down a smooth scale. It's an idle thing. Edna can't help but wonder if this is how a million little things begin to fall apart, not out of maliciousness, but out of distraction.

Edna follows the young woman down the street, oscillating between strangers, consumed by the feeling of swimming upstream. The overcast sky spits down on them. She has known this woman only an hour, maybe less, and she is following her now, slightly too close and slightly too fast, on a street that she barely recognizes. This woman is moving quickly, she knows, because she is desperate to get her dream back. For better or worse it is still her dream and perhaps she has slept in a vacuum for a week now. Sleep without dreams, without this specific dream as though locked into a purgatory forever waiting in the hollowness of a sleeping brain that refuses to entertain itself with a fumbled montage of scenes cobbled together from a day's fragments. Divorced from reinterpretations and translations of events big and small. Peccadillo and triumph.

The lobby of the old apartment building has the thick smell of must and the combined cooking of hundreds of past and present tenants, diffused into something like two-day old Chinese food left on the kitchen counter.

The woman turns key in lock and the apartment reveals itself: cluttered with hanging tapestries and mismatched furniture that looks as though it was salvaged from street corners and garage sales. It's a college student's apartment. A girl barely older than Liam. It is homie without feeling claustrophobic. A dream catcher hangs mockingly in front of a broad window.

The women lie timidly on the bed, side-by-side like strangers suddenly aware they are sitting too close to each other in an empty movie theater. It is impossible to tell how long this will take. Edna inhales the stranger's unfamiliar smell. A mixture of sweat and dusky perfume. Slowly they are drawn into the relative gravity of each other, forming on oroboros of dreams.

We Live Here Now

My kid sister Phoebe stood in the doorway of the cheap motel staring into the dimness. Cubby, her stuffed bear, dangled from her five-year-old hand, his butt hanging a fraction of an inch above the crinkled gray paint of the outdoor hallway. It's one of those indelible moments that will be forever painted on the inside of my eyelids.

"S'this?" She asked.

"Our home," I said.

I channeled every possible sentiment of good nature I'd ever witnessed, but never felt. I squeezed past her and ran my hand up and down the wall until I found the switch. The warm orange glow of the table lamps didn't seem to make her feel any better. Phoebs took a few reluctant steps into the room. She was still wearing her scuffed pink slippers. The dingy fake fur at the ankle was worn into a threadbare fold. She hugged Cubby to her chest, his button eyes regarding me suspiciously.

"See," I said.

"It isn't a home."

"It sure is," I said, "it's our home. It's yours and mine and Cubby and Mama's."

Ma was out at the van grabbing our bags. Suitcases clattered on asphalt, and I could hear her cursing into the evening humidity.

"It's not even a 'partment."

"It's just like an apartment," I set my duffle on the floor, "In fact, it's even better than a 'partment."

Mom thumped up the steps, the metal railing pinged as the suitcases hit it. I picked Phoebs up and half-flung onto the far bed, where she bounced to a stop without ever letting go of Cubby. Ma appeared in the doorway suitcases dangling from each hand. I may forget the day of the week, or the name of the place, or whether the soap was in little rectangular packages or little round packages – but I will never forget that image of her.

"Great," she said.

"Is there more?" I asked.

"Phoebs, brush teeth."

"Want me to get anything else from the van?"

"This isn't even a 'partment."

"Teeth."

The door stood open to the late summer and the heat came through in waves, shimmering the street lights into blurred halos. The suitcases were piled on the carpet at Ma's feet. I picked up Phoebe's pink roller suitcase and dug out the Ziploc with her toothbrush and glittery toothpaste.

"Listen to Ma," I said.

"I'll be back," Ma said.

"Where are you going *now*?" Phoebs whined.

"I'm going to the store." Ma was looking at me but talking to Phoebs, "Carl can grab you a snack from the vending machine."

"I'm 'posed to do teeth."

"Pick something out. Then teeth."

Ma fished a crumpled wad of cash from her wallet and held it out. As I grabbed the bills she held them fast and pulled me close. With our faces inches apart she mouthed: *I don't have to tell you.*

And she didn't.

Down in the parking lot I heard the van start and pulled back the heavy curtains in time to watch Ma ease onto the otherwise empty street. She'd be gone a while. She wasn't going to the store; she was going to get blind drunk.

Phoebs sat on the bed with her arms around Cubby. I looked at the wad of cash in my hand. I'd seen a row of glass-fronted vending machines on the ground floor next to the rumbling icemaker. I hoisted Phoebs to my hip and walked down the stairs. The staticky sound of cicadas electrified the middle distance. I set Phoebs in front of the machines and she examined her options. The stink of industrial cleaners and melting tar loitered among the cars.

"S'that one?"

"Peanut Butter cups."

She pointed to another.

"Milk Duds," I said, "Carmel with chocolate on the outside."

"Skittles?"

I looked. "Yeah, they have Skittles."

I lifted her up and she fed the dollar into the machine and punched the buttons. The thunk of the package made me wince. Phoebs squatted in front of the machine and I pressed back the plastic door. She peered into that pocket of darkness and grabbed the package. Back in the room she curled under the blankets as I opened the package for her and found cartoons on TV. She looked miniature on the king sized bed; the wrapper crumpled as she fished out several Skittles at a time. Cubby sat beside her, the shadow of the two of them morphing into a glob of round bear ears and little girl ponytail. The smell of stale cigarettes and dust had been ground into the carpet. The AC chugged along behind me, prickling Goosebumps along my arms and neck. I stared down at my backpack and gently nudged it into the corner with my toe.

    The room was one more unfamiliar place in a growing chain. Everything was a rental for us: apartments, falling apart houses, motel rooms. Other than a long winter we spent with Ma's parents, we'd never lived anywhere long; never owned anything other than two cars and our clothes. North Carolina, West Virginia, Kentucky, Tennessee. We'd lived a dozen different places before Ma landed a job at the hospital in Virginia. That spring we lived in a brick rambler, tucked back off Grandin Road. By mid-May the heat settled in, pressing humid hands down on our shoulders. Ma's worked nights, opposite of Pops, and most days she left right after he got home. If she left before he got home it was no doubt because of the argument I'd heard through the bedroom walls.

Going into the basement was *verboten*. Pops disappeared down there for hours at a time, often right after dinner. Thin wooden stairs that led down into the basement seemed as if they'd barely support you. It was a late weekday afternoon when, mostly to escape the heat, I ventured into the smell of mildew, spilled beer, and sweat. At the bottom of the stairs a chain dangled from a single bare bulb. Along the far wall was an old workbench. Tools and faded porno mags littered the scarred wooden surface. Behind the workbench, tacked to the wall, was a tattered Rebel Flag. Off to one side an old rag covered something bulky.

I grabbed a corner of the cloth and folded it back. Underneath was a pistol I didn't know Pops owned. I sat down on a barstool near the workbench to examine the thing. It was heavier than I expected. The dull metal shined in the stark light as I turned it over in my hands, running my thumb along the crisp edges.

I hadn't heard his truck pull up or the front door open. Through the opened door I could hear the TV playing. But there he was, standing at the top of the stairs with a beer in each hand.

"You piece of shit," he said starting down the steps.

He was so focused on me he forgot to duck under a low ceiling beam. His head cracked against it and he tumbled backwards onto the steps. His beer cans skittered across the concrete as he groped for the railing, swinging one arm up to keep his balance. His hand smacked against the dangling bulb and the chain rattled as the light swung back and forth casting hideous shadows on the cement. It looked like someone turned on a red faucet above him. I never thought a person could bleed so much.

"Piece of shit," he said.

One of his eyes was squinted closed. He looked from me to the blood on his hand, edging towards me like a drunk in a darkened room. I moved out of reach, backing up until I was against the brick wall. Pops placed one hand on the workbench and sat on the barstool. An entire galaxy of blood stretched across the floor.

"Get a towel," he said.

I didn't move. He was leaning forward, his hands pressed to his head as he grimaced. The tendons and muscles of his back stretched the black cursive letters of *Donnelly Construction* from shoulder to shoulder. Dribbles of blood curved down his cheek and neck. He leaned so far forward that the back legs of the chair hovered above the floor. I counted the rhythm as he rocked slowly forward and back. As he took deep breaths his shirt stretched and went slack. I took a step forward and hooked my toe under the crosspiece of the stool. I waited. The legs inched upwards. I kicked hard. The chair came out from under him and his chin smacked the workbench. His head ricocheted backwards. His body bounced against the concrete.

The light bulb slowed to a soft, lazy circle. The chair splintered beneath him, one of the legs snapped off and landed across the room. He laid there motionless. A bubble of spit and blood expanded and contracted on his lips. The silence of the basement settled in as I stared down at him, the gun gripped tightly in my hand. I backed up the stairs. In the kitchen I set the gun gingerly on the counter; the image the gun bent and distorted in the chrome finish of the toaster. Phoebs stood in the hallway; behind her in the living room I could hear the babble of cartoons.

"S'that," she pointed to the gun.

"Nothing."

"I want juice."

My kid sister pulled back a chair and clambered up. Numbly I walked to the refrigerator and opened the door. The humming coolness of the refrigerator chilled the sweat on my forehead as I bent down. Phoebs hummed one of those kids' songs from TV. I poured her apple juice and set it in front of her. Grasping the cup in both hands she tilted her head back, swallowed, and finally gasped when she the cup was empty. I listened to her slippered feet scuff down the hallway to the TV. She sat cross-legged in front of the TV with Cubby at her side. The gun sat on the counter and as I reached towards it I could see my hand shaking.

Each creaking step into the basement was louder than the last. I braced one hand on the low ceiling beam and ducked under. Pops was lying on his back in the middle of the room. The bubble of spit and blood had popped, speckling his lips with pink froth. He made a little groaning noise, but didn't move. I took a few steps forward and crouched down, listening to his shallow breathing. I wasn't sure if I was happy he was alive.

From the kitchen phone I called Ma at work and told her Pops had fallen down the stairs. She asked me if he was conscious, and if he was breathing. She told me to hang up and call 911. Phoebs came down the hall again as I stood there on the phone with the dispatcher. I hung up we stood there in the thick, stale heat of the kitchen. The weight of the gun dragged me towards the ground. Without much thought I opened the freezer and set the pistol on a bag of frozen peas, pressing it down as the metal fogged over.

When they arrived I led the paramedics to the top of the stairs. The lights of the ambulance lacked urgency. As the two men trundled down the stairs with their boxes, my sister hid behind my arm, pulling it around her. Her tiny weight pressed against my leg; her clammy hands twisted around mine as we stood in the kitchen. The men bent over Pops and talked to each other in casual voices. Ma got home as they loaded him onto the gurney. She stood in the kitchen with her keys in her hand, her gray hair curled in heavy waves across her scalp. I could see the heavy lines etched into her face. She wanted to know how bad it was. She told them she was a nurse.

"He's stable," one of the men said as they wheeled Pops past.

Pops looked at me around the oxygen mask with nothing but shear and absolute hatred. Ma, Phoebs, and I stood on the front steps as they loaded the gurney into the back of the ambulance. We watched as they pulled away. Ma led us inside and closed the front door. The TV was still playing in the next room. She looked at the two of us there in the narrow doorway. Phoebs hadn't let go of my hand since the paramedics arrived. Ma turned and walked down the hallway to the bedroom.

Over her shoulder she said: "Start packing,"

Phoebs fell asleep just after midnight. Ma wasn't back yet, and I didn't expect her anytime soon. I turned off the TV and tugged the edge of the covers over my sister. She hadn't brushed her teeth, but I figured it didn't much matter. I took off my shirt, the fabric was damp from sweat and cold from the AC. I shivered as I wrapped myself in the scratchy wool blanket.   The floor was hard and the room was so dark I could barely see anything; light from the parking lot bled through the curtains. I could hear Phoebs snoring on the other side of the room. I imagined a hospital bed somewhere. Pops connected to a tangle and tubes and wires. Ma in a back road tavern with a Boiler Maker and a cigarette. A whole new chain of rentals. New states. New schools. Nothing would change. I stared at the ceiling and listened to the drone of the AC. Rolling over I reached out and placed a hand on my bag, feeling the contour of the pistol beneath the canvas.

They Say

It's early fall when I first see into their apartment. Stubborn clusters of amber leaves cling to the elm trees between the buildings. That night I turn off the kitchen lights and dry my hands on the dishtowel and watch the blue flicker of TV highlight their faces like an electrical storm. I've heard that we're only truly ourselves when no one else is looking. Maybe that's when self-consciousness is subtracted from actions and we stumble across ourselves without realizing it.

For days afterwards I stand at the window in my darkened kitchen staring into their apartment, catching glimpses of shuffling feet; a shoulder; a sliver of torso. I'm an accidental voyeur turned intentional.

Because I have no other frame of reference I name the man George and the woman Tina. He is tall and lanky, his dark hair often tousled. She is short, olive complexioned. Something makes me think she speaks with an accent – Spanish or French – with round, liquid vowels.

I watch their scattered conversations as they crane their necks to lift their voices across the room. They turn off the kitchen sink to listen, speak brief sentences and turn the sink back on. They stack dishes beside the sink to dry. They sit on the couch folding clothes. For long stretches of time they say nothing. They occupy the same space, filled only with rambling TV conversations that make up for their silence.

Perhaps they moved in during the Spring or Summer when the trees were blocking my view. Perhaps things were different for them then. It's hard to imagine that things for them might have ever been different from how they are now.

When the apartment is empty I am consumed by thoughts of where they might be. I imagine George works in sales. Most of the day his ear is glued to a phone and he nearly shouts that he has to have 500 widgets by Friday, and no, no he can't wait, and these guys keep dicking him around.

Tina, I imagine, works at a gym; she leaves the apartment in a tank top and black workout pants, carrying a water bottle and a gym bag. Maybe she teaches yoga. She stands at the front of a room full of women. A mirror behind her reflects the students and pale hardwood floor.

Tina says: today we're going to start with the-such-and-such pose. Breathe. Feel your chakras.

I can hear only the muted tones of angry voices; syllables are absorbed by the mosaic of leaves plastered to the pavement separating us. The distance is too great to read anything other than gestures and intonation. Each word has its own barometric pressure.

Tina says to George: You never do the fucking dishes.

And George says: Why should I do the fucking dishes? You're the woman.

I'm the fucking woman, so I do the dishes?
You do the fucking dishes. I mow the lawn.
We don't have a lawn.

In December light fog washes out the city and subtracts depth and details from the distant trees and mountains. A sheet of white paper has been slipped behind the buildings. The world ceases to exist.

On every corner a red suited Santa rings a bell or shakes a tambourine. All through the city are signs of the holidays. Traffic clogs downtown streets. People haul massive shopping bags. Reindeer antlers suction to car windows. Wreaths are attached to the front of cars. The City tangles strings of lights around lampposts. People huddle in jackets and scarves, folding in on themselves like human origami in the metallic cold of the city.

I watch as Tina wraps a grayish box that is either an electric razor or a camera. She wraps a sweater, which she folds and refolds before laying it in a box and wrapping it with curlicue bows. In the store she held this sweater at arm's length, squinting to picture it on George.

George stands in a bookstore, picking up one book and then another, flipping them over to read the back. Thumbing through the pages for pictures. He asks an employee what his wife would like. She's a yoga teacher; she likes true crime books.

Tina disappears shortly after the New Year. The desiccated Christmas tree –
a Noble Fir or Norway Spruce – sits by the curb. Boxes are stacked by the front door. George has melted into a routine comprised of walking, sitting, and standing as necessity dictates. Pizza boxes and beer bottles create a calendar of the days she's been gone. He paces the apartment with the phone pressed to his ear; I am certain he is talking to Tina. He sits immobile on the couch thinking of Tina.

I have lost interest.

Potential Truth

I.

"Don't leave anything out," she says, "even if it's painful."

"It's a lot to remember," he says.

She burrows her face into his shoulder, her fingers moving like contented breath along the muscle to the hollow of his neck. The warm cocoon of blankets is bunched around them. His mind is already calling up memories and recreating the ghost of a thousand former conversations.

"Of course you can't tell me everything," she says, "no one could do that – remember everything."

"Telling the thing would take longer than the real thing," he says.

"Your version will be enough."

II.

He tries to find a specific access point – a place into the true memory, the memory that is closest to how things actually happened. Not only for her, but for himself. He wants to get it as right as he can. Even so, he knows something will be intentionally or unintentionally left out (either for his sake or for hers or, maybe, for both of them). He will leave something out to save her from heartache or save himself from embarrassment. He knows he will end up backtracking, fumbling for the best possible version of the truth.

III.

    The bed they are lying in belongs to her. The pillows, the sheets, the bookcases, the half empty wine glasses – all of it belongs to her. Other than his memories few things here are his. In the late afternoon dimness, the sagging sun is the only thing that gives some indication of time. His brain stutter-skips on the words ephemeral and intangible, although he's not sure he could pin down the actual definition of either word. He stares at the semi-familiar surroundings trying to orient himself. The bookshelf across the room is filled with her battered paperbacks; he tries not to think about ownership.

IV.

    "Take your time," she says.
    He searches the ceiling for a waypoint – scanning the blankness of the roughly textured paint. His heart races. Has the room darkened by degrees? It could be only a cloud elbowing its way in front of the sun. The darkening of the room is the only minute hand they have. The calling up of the memory has become an alchemical change – a transmutation of self spurred by a backwards drift into memory.

V.

Even now, as he pauses between one word and the next, he is uncertain how much of what he is telling her is truth. He is moving and not moving – engaged in the intimate time travel of memory. He tries to settle his eyes in a neutral place, where the past lurks teasingly, and then he knows that he has cornered himself in his own lies. He questions the veracity of his story even as the syllables fall from his lips. Even as his mouth forms words and sentences – tracing ever more intricate lies that ripple towards the high ceiling of her apartment.

VI.

When he finishes the story as much as he is capable of finishing it he is suddenly aware that she is still lying beside him. Although she has barely made a sound he knows without looking that there are tears on her face. It is as if he is everywhere and nowhere as the silence returns to the room; there isn't so much as an echo of the last word. And yet the end of the story rings in his ears.

"It's not easy to digest," she says.

And he thinks *digest* is a strange choice of words. A word more appropriate for a home cooked meal – something carefully prepared and hand fed to her; but it has upset her stomach, and now the belly ache is the result of half-truth or whole truth or quarter truth, or some other, unknown and infinitesimally small fraction of truth.

VII.

By the time that he leaves her apartment it's well past sunset and the streets are clogged with traffic. Outside, in the cool familiarity of yesterday's clothes, he tries to work out the complexity of the evening. He tells himself it was the right thing to do, even though he isn't sure whether it was the right thing for her or for him. Just now there is only the visceral, the gut, the intuition – divorced from the cut and dry emotions so often parceled into brackets and boxes.

Off the Tracks

The car jerked like we'd gone over a pothole, a metallic noise rocking the left side of the car from the front to back. We'd been headed down Highway 11 out towards Snohomish, just me and Graham. My brother and I had become closer since he became a frosh and I'd become a senior at Olympic View High. I don't know what we were talking about, probably nothing – just listening to music, windows down, cruising down the highway.

When that sound hit I pulled off the road my hands fixed to the wheel, Graham twisted in his seat and looked over his shoulder and said he thought we hit something. I got out of the car and told him to stay put. The body was about fifty yards back, tossed in a ditch. As I got closer I could hear the ugly, animal struggle for breath, the body barely resembling a cat anymore.

I straddled the ditch and stepped down into the dirt, which gave under my feet – that soft squishing feeling of semi-dried mud. The bugs irritated the air around my head, and the animal's inside muck mixed with the clay-like earth turning everything murky black. The grating noise of the cat coaxed Graham out of the car, and he moved closer until his shadow bent down and over the ditch.

"That a cat?" he asked.

"Was."

"It's still alive," he goes, "so it *is* a cat."

"Well, it's a moot point, kiddo, he isn't going to last a whole lot longer."

"We should take him to a vet."

"First," I said, "I think it's a she. Second, what vet? We're like a hundred miles from anything."

"So you killed a fucking cat."

I felt bad that he had said that, you're supposed to say nice things at a time like that. It was pretty bad. Graham stepped into the ditch on the other side of the cat and crouched down. He looked at it seriously for a second, his hands on his knees, his eyes squinted against the sun. Grabbing a nearby branch, he pointed at the guts coming out the cat's side. I moved around next to Graham as he reached forward, and turned over the animal's nametag with the branch. The cat's collar and tag were covered with too bright blood, but as Graham leaned closer he could make out the etched letters.

"Oscar," he said, "you killed Oscar the cat."

"He's not dead."

"You said yourself he will be."

The mewling got louder. The cat's head rested against the side of the ditch and it watched us with light green eyes. Turning over the tag had startled the cat, but it really didn't have any choice except to lie there and die. Graham climbed up on the other side of the ditch, hacking at the dry underbrush with the stick and pushing the grass back with the toes of his mismatched Converse. He bent down and picked up a hunk of gray asphalt the size of a softball that had somehow broken free from the road. He jumped back across the ditch and handed me the thing. We couldn't leave the cat there, it wouldn't be right to leave the animal there to die slowly in the ditch, alone in the hot sun. Graham held out the asphalt, and I took it in both hands without looking at him, stepped down into the ditch, made eye contact with Oscar before stepping up on the pavement and around to the other side where he wouldn't be able to see me.

    I inched closer, scooting along until my toes touched the carnage. I turned the rock over in my hands trying for the best grip, settling on a grip that kept one of the edges pointed downwards. That wail kept going, the mottled gray fur of his side rising and falling in really deep breaths. I was squatting behind him, holding the rock over my head. The cat was breathing heavy – so was I – our breathing was almost in unison, the sun clinging to the back of my neck. Graham was watching to see if I'd really do the thing.

    I hit him just to one side of his head, near his left ear. The rock slipped in my hands cutting a gash at the base of my thumb. I cursed and Oscar made a noise louder and worse than before. I wish I could explain that noise, like screeching metal and cats in heat and pure grief. Little bits of fur stuck to the edge of the rock, and the skin was just peeled back over his tiny skull. I raised the rock again and again and again and again. The blows blurred together. I'm sure that I had my eyes closed. It must have taken five or six blows to finally kill him, and when I was done I sat back on the edge of the ditch, and laid the rock down beside me. Below me in the ditch was a mess of blood and fur and blackish mud. I stood up, my back aching, and little dots of white in front of my eyes.

Graham looked down at me, and helped me up onto the pavement, hauling me up with both hands and leaning back against my weight. I wiped my hands on my jeans, turned, and walked back to the car, which seemed farther away than I remembered. Graham stood there looking down at Oscar. I had to shout at him to tell him to get back in the damn car already. By the time he got back to the car I was sitting with the engine idling, staring down the road. A pickup swished passed us, rocking the car as Graham slammed the door.

"Fuck," Graham goes after a while, "that was intense."

"Shut up," I said.

"Smacksmacksmack," he said, "brutal."

"Shut up,"

"Smacksmack," he said.

"Drop it." I said.

"I'm just saying, Trev, that's insane."

"Graham? Graham. Shut up, Graham."

When we got to Tyler's house we were already about a half hour later than we were supposed to be. The rest of the drive I kept the needle under thirty-five, leaning forward so that my chest almost touched the steering wheel. I knew that before they got inside he would be telling Tyler all about how his big brother had just killed a cat, first running over it, then smashing its skull with a rock.

    Back at home I squatted in front of the car and stared at the bumper and the wheels. There wasn't so much as a mark on the car. I showered and changed and went to work at Movie Stars. I couldn't focus. It was busy and people were asking me about films I knew like the back of my hand. There wasn't much to say, not even about the films that I loved – I figured they could smell the blood. Even strangers, it seemed, smiling children and spotty-faced teens could tell that I had killed another living thing.

    At closing time, I checked out a stack of war movies and flung them on the backseat of my car. Somehow, I hoped, the movies would allow me to desensitize myself to that shit. After all, what was one cat to all the men that died at Normandy, or all the big-tittied blonds killed in horror movies? There had to be some way to put it all in perspective. For hours I watched movies on the little TV in our bedroom. On screen soldiers lost limbs. Killers in leather masks eviscerated sorority girls. I fast-forwarded to the most violent scenes that I could find. Gallons of fake blood washed over the small screen. When I figured mom was asleep I poured some of her Franzia into an empty coke bottle and moved up to the living room. Mom was no doubt too drunk to hear the sounds of death, the pleas for help, the cries of pain, the explosions, and the chainsaws. If she woke up she ignored the sounds. In all honesty it wouldn't have been all that strange, since I watched these movies more often than anything. Usually it was just for kicks, that little shot of adrenaline, rooting for the bad guy; that sort of thing. But that night it wasn't because of the carnage, or the real brutality. It had something to do with the cat. Even though it seemed like it shouldn't have been such a big deal.

    I couldn't really sleep until it was starting to get light outside. I finally fell asleep out – being just exhausted from the day, from work and all that. Around one the next afternoon I woke up when Graham got home from Tyler's and came into our room and sat down on my bed. He was holding something in his hand, and when I sat up he handed me Oscar's collar. Graham's battered Army surplus jacket was torn at the left elbow, and I could smell earth and night air on him. The faint sweat smell on his skin. He just sat there holding out the collar to me and smiling. He jingled the tags in my face and when I didn't take it he dropped it into my lap. There were patches of blood soaked into that blue nylon, and little bits of fur stuck to the edges.

    "You're sick, you know that?" I reached down and picked up the collar and dropped it on the nightstand. My hands felt oily with grime that I'm sure wasn't really there. It was a too sudden reminder that yesterday had really happened after all – that it hadn't been some nightmare.

    Graham waited for me as I got up and got dressed, throwing a tennis ball at the wall at the foot of his bed. The ball thumped and rebounded back to his hand. When I was dressed he followed me upstairs and sat watching me as I poured a bowl of cereal. He said he wanted to go to Japanese Gulch, the woods behind the old post office. I didn't want to go, but Graham can be pretty damn persistent sometimes, and he knew I liked it there, walking through the woods and hopping trains down to the beach. He stood waiting as I tied my shoes and pulled on an old hoodie.

It was hotter than it had been the day before. At the corner we cut back behind the post office and down the hill towards the trail-head. Neither of us said anything, and there was really nothing that I could think of. Maybe in some way I was just waiting for Graham to say something, to show his hand, to give me a clue. His dark brown hair flopped in front of his eyes, and he brushed it back, proud that it was almost long enough to tuck behind his ears.

Usually we crossed the creek wherever we could find a log or some stones or whatever to walk across. On the other side of the creek you have to scramble up this steep bank and push your way through sticker bushes and nettles, but after that you're pretty much on the tracks and can smell the oily creosote of the railroad. I started walking down the tracks towards the beach and Graham followed balancing on the metal rail closest to me, his arms out at his sides making a show out of it, turning his mouth into a wide O.

"Tyler think that shit with the cat was cool?"

"He's already afraid of you."

"Afraid of me?"

"He thinks seniors are Jason Bourne or some shit."

Graham dropped off the rail with an exaggerated fall, flailing his arms wildly and stooping forward it looked like he would face plant right there. After recovering his balance, he swerved towards me, punched my arm and sprinted ahead. When I didn't chase him right away he stopped and turned back to me, walking backwards in the crunchcrunch of gravel.

"Let's kill something else," he goes.

"Shut up Graham."

"A bird, or a squirrel, something small. We can put it on the tracks and the train'll hit it."

"That's messed up, kid."

"You're messed up, man, you look in the mirror like ever?"

He turned around and kept walking, we were headed more or less towards Devil's Peak, the place we'd used as a fort since I was his age. Really it was just a clearing at the top of a hill, a place where we'd camped a few times last summer with some of my friends – friends who pretty much tolerated Graham because they'd known him for so damned long, and besides they liked to see him drunk on Steele Reserve, smoking cigarettes like a fiend. He was a little ahead of me now, working his way up the hill, using saplings and roots to pull himself up. Near the top we'd strung a piece of yellow rope round a tree and knotted a heavy branch to one end, that way you could pull yourself up that last little bit into the clearing.

It was pretty much how we left it: a few old milk crates turned over by the fire pit, an old side mirror from some junker car tied to a tree, names and curses carved into the trees, dented beer cans half buried in mud and leaves. The wind was picking up and I sat down on one of the crates as Graham walked around and around, picking bark off of the trees and flinging branches out into the undergrowth.

"How would we catch something anyways," I finally said.

Graham shrugged and kicked one of the crates closer to the fire pit, looking disappointed. Finally, he turned over the crate and sat down.

"I didn't realize you were such a pussy."

"Yeah?" I asked.

"You should have seen yourself. About to cry."

"Okay."

"Poor little kitty. I don't want to kill you. Smashsmashsmash. What was that like, man? Intense right?"

"Shut up, Graham."

"Shut up, Graham. Graham, I'm a fucking flower over here, don't tease me."

"I'm fucking warning you."

Graham jumped up pulling his milk crate with him as he stood and flinging the thing at me so that an arc of dirt and mud shot up in the air and spiraled after it. His aim was off and it passed me and somersaulted into the tree behind me rattling the branches as it went. He was standing there with his arms at his sides and his head down a little, then he started laughing. I stood up spreading my feet in anticipation, and winged a flattened beer can at him – which just missed to one side as he leaned out of the way.

"Easy killer." He said.

I was waiting for him to make his move, since he always made the first move. He was predictable like that, and when he finally did it was just a bum rush with his arms out like a half-blind defensive tackle. I mean Graham wasn't a very big guy, just a five-foot-nothing freshman, but I braced myself and he caught me mid stomach and as he hit me I turned and pushed his shoulders at the same time so that he spun to the side and back and hit the ground in a little tumble and lie there not move. I stood there waiting for him to get up, but I knew that he was fine. After a minute or so I walked and nudged him with my shoe. His eyes were closed and he was limp.

I pressed my foot onto his shoulder and gave him a little push. Graham rolled over onto his back and looked up at me. He folded his hands on his stomach and looked up at me. There was all sorts of shit clinging to his hair and his jacket – dried mud, little branches and leaves.

"What, no rock?" He said.
"You gave me the rock, kid."

"Right," he said standing up, "let me find you one."

But Graham didn't move. He stood there about an arm's length away from me, his breath coming heavier now and I was expecting him to charge at me again. He cracked a little smile and picked something from his lower lip, a little bit of grit or dirt.Turning away from him I walked back towards the yellow rope, expecting at any moment to feel his clumsy, full-body tackle. When I got to the edge, I slid down, using one hand to break and then did a little jog at the foot of hill to slow myself into a walk, and made my way towards the tracks.

When I looked back I didn't see him coming down the slope as I expected, and now it seemed like he could be anywhere up there in the bushes. Near the slope up to the trail out I heard a train coming and I sat back behind the stickers and watched it pass, thinking that as soon as it was gone Graham would be standing there on the other side. I should have known that when the train finished passing Graham wouldn't be there. I turned and walked home, figuring that maybe he'd caught the train to the beach, and that when he got bored he'd head home.

When it was starting to get dark he hadn't shown up yet, I told Mom that he was staying over at Tyler's again. Mom shrugged and stepped out onto the porch to have another Virginia Slim, sipping her glass of wine and staring at the traffic down on the Speedway. At dusk you could see the brake lights headed south and the white headlights headed north. She would sit out there for hours thinking about who knows what. If she gave a shit it never showed. I stood there for a while staring at her through the kitchen window, and then went down to our room. Graham showed up a little after ten. I was sitting on my bed rewatching Night of the Living Dead for the millionth time.

"Come here," he said.
"Why?"
"Just fucking come here," he said.

I pushed myself up from the bed and put my shoes on, I left the movie playing in the background, since I figured that whatever he wanted wouldn't take long. At the sliding door to the backyard, he turned on the patio light, and pointed at a grocery bag on the cement.

"The fuck's that?"
"Check it out for yourself, pussy."

I opened the sliding door and stepped onto the patio. The night was cool, and there was a little breeze that was rippling the plastic bag – something heavy held it down, so only the handles rustled against each other. Down on the Speedway someone gunned their engine and the guttural sound turned into an earsplitting whine. I squatted beside the bag and pushed it open with my finger. Something furry and dead was at the bottom of the bag. I closed the bag and stood up, turning to look at my brother. He stood there grinning. Graham reached into the front pocket of his jacket, fished out a bent Virginia Slim and lit it with a Zippo I'd stolen for him from the gas station.

"That Oscar?" I went.

"Nope," he said, "that's a fresh one just for you."

I picked up the bag and carried it to the trashcan around the side of the house and dropped the thing in. Whatever it was thumped to the bottom of the can and I let the lid slam down. Leaning against the house, Graham followed me with his eyes, sucking hard on the filter. I walked inside not looking at him, turned off the patio light, and slid the door closed. Oscar's collar was on my nightstand. I pitched it into the garbage, went upstairs to find something to eat. Mom was passed out on the couch again. It must have been a weekend night. The rest of the week she usually went to bed early-ish, so she could get down to the supermarket for her nine-hour shift in the meat department. She was snoring a little, the TV playing some too cheerful infomercial. Her robe was twisted up over her legs and the comforter was tangled up on the floor. I shook out the comforter and draped it over her.

Graham was still in bed when I got up for work in the morning. I didn't feel like telling anyone about my weekend. Not about the cat or the fight out at Japanese Gulch or the collar. Denise, the girl I worked with, teased me for playing comedies all day.

"The fuck got into you?" She hopped up on the counter next to me.

"Just need a little levity."

"Double points. SAT word."

Denise was a decent enough looking girl, and we'd gotten drunk a few times and made out in the back of my car. But that was about it. She was more like a sister, I guess. We gave each other shit, but probably actually cared about each other.

"I'm not staying here," I hoped down at straightened a stack of DVDs.

"That's fair."

"I mean, I got to get out of this shitty city."

"You get weirder by the day."

I took my time getting home. I was trying to figure out what to do about Graham. Figuring out how to give my kid brother advice when he was, at the same time, scaring the shit out of me, seemed a little dicey. It's not like I could tell mom. What would I tell her? That her youngest son was a fuck up and potential sociopath? There was no way to really make it make sense to her, and even if it did make sense to her, I sort of doubted that there was anything that she would want to do about it.

When I got home I found Graham sitting in our bedroom, tossing his ball at the wall. In a stack of loose newspaper I could see that he'd cut dozens of obituaries out of the paper and tacked them to the wall beside his bed above his bed. He didn't say anything when I came in. He just kept tossing that ball at the wall, that repetitive thumpthump as a changed out of my work clothes and headed upstairs to find something to eat. Mom was fussing with a box of Mac'n'Cheese. Her skin was dry and red from having spent the day out on the porch with a pack of Virginia Slims and a box of Franzia. From our house you could see a pretty decent sunset from the back porch. Maybe that was one of the things that she enjoyed. Who the hell knows.

"I'll finish this," I told her, opening the packet of powdered cheese and pouring it into a measuring cup to mix with milk and butter. Mom made her way into the living room and I could hear her flipping through the channels until she found something she liked.

"Your brother here?" She called from the couch.

"Downstairs."

I finished the Mac and carried a bowl out to mom, refilled her wine. In the kitchen I snagged a few of her Slims from the pack and palmed them as I poured my share of wine into a glass and carried my own plate downstairs. The wall beside the stairs was cool to the touch, and I tried to press my weight down on the steps as hard as I could so that Graham would know that I was coming. I craned my neck around the corner into our bedroom, half expecting Graham to attack me as I looked into the room, but he wasn't there. The sheets on his bed were messed up, and there were dirt and mud stains on the blankets. Little piles of dirt and gravel showed where he'd set his shoes the night before. I checked the closet and the downstairs bathroom and finally walked outside to into the backyard. The sun was down and the sky was a tangeriney orange at the edges. The breeze kicked up, carrying highway sounds up to our backyard.

I went back in and sat down next to Mom on the couch, "he must have gone out."

"Apple didn't fall far from the tree on that one," she said.

I waited up with her that night, watching Law and Order, and hoping that Graham would be asleep by the time I made my way down to the bedroom. Around two Mom passed out, and I went downstairs, leaving the TV playing.

The wine had made my mouth dry and sticky, and I weaved a little as I made my way down the stairs. I guess I hadn't heard Graham come in but from the light in the hall I could see Graham lying on his bed. As soon as I lie down Graham was mewling like a dying animal. I threw both of my pillows at him, but it wasn't until I hit him with one of my shoes that he stopped. In the morning the collar was on my nightstand again, and Graham was gone. I carried the collar out to the garbage and buried it beneath banana peels and wadded up tissues.

I thought maybe I would wake up to that collar again, but I didn't want to have anything else to do with it. It bothered me more that Graham was preoccupied with the thing, than the actual act of killing Oscar. It was right, wasn't it? What else could

I have done? It would have been heartless to leave the cat laying there, dying alone. It was mercy.

Graham kept to himself that week. That weekend Tyler's mom had called to say that we needed to come pick him up, because he'd just gotten in a fight with Tyler. When I got there, Graham's lip was busted and his eye was swelling shut. Tyler's mom just stood on the front porch with her arms crossed and watched me pull up. I barely had my door open when Graham jogged over and got in the car. He looked like hell, and I wasn't sure if there was anything I could say or do to comfort him. I swear I thought he was going to cry but the kid held himself together. I've never wanted to play the dad. I wasn't about to start now. I waited as he drew the seatbelt across his stomach and clicked it into place.

The drive was quick and quiet, and I coasted up into our driveway and cut the engine. We sat there in the silence of the car, the engine ticking. Graham unbuckled his belt. Dried blood had collected at the corner of his mouth and etched a deep line on his lip. He had his door opened partway and was easing out of the seat when I told him to go inside and clean his face up before mom saw him.

Mom could be unpredictable with this shit. Dad used to beat the fuck out of her whenever he felt like it, and seeing Graham bruised up like that wouldn't have been very good for any of us. Mom just asked me where he was, and I told her that he must have been up late, and it looked like he was going to bed. She shrugged and asked me to go get her another pack of cigarettes from the freezer. When she was drunk enough that she'd stopped making sense I went downstairs. Graham was asleep in his clothes, his jacket drawn close around him.

    In the morning he paraded around the house like a tough guy, wearing his black-eyed souvenir with pride. I tried to hang out with him, but he was being a dick, so I gave up. Late in the afternoon he put on his shoes and jacket and walked outside, probably on his way down to the Gulch. I tried not to imagine him out there, slinking through the bushes, trying to catch something small to kill, or setting fire to the underbrush. When he came back, just after dusk, he smelled like sweat and dirt, and I could smell the cigarettes on him. He pushed the covers off of his bed; lie down on the bare mattress. After I got in bed and turned out the lamp on my nightstand, the whole room was thick darkness and there was the ticking of my alarm clock.   Over there – across the room – I heard him move on his mattress, and I knew that he was awake. I could feel him starring at the ceiling, trying to control his breathing.

This Endless Road

    The overnight Greyhound out of San Antonio is a piss smelling thing crowded with the misery of the ten thousand people who have worn the seats threadbare over the years. Rita has been unable to sleep, and by the time the bus stops in a nowhere town somewhere in New Mexico, she drags herself from precarious half-sleep. She's starving and the only thing open at six in the morning is a diner a half block from the bus depot, one of those places obligated to spring up along the highway at nearly perfect intervals, all vinyl booths and syrup stained tables that might as well have been pre-manufactured. She sits at the long counter next to the only other patron, a middle aged trucker types whose face has been carved and eroded by time and wind and sun. It's a face eroded by the loneliness of the open road, she thinks, and is half-surprised at herself when she strikes up a conversation, not pausing to consider what she's saying. Perhaps it's the particular nature of the stress and exhaustion that prompts her to spool out white lie after white lie. And suddenly she is telling him that she is headed to Seattle to see her brother – but the place is no place that she has ever been. It's simply a place that seems unfathomably different from the arid, nearly treeless landscape of the Southwest. And so, she's just as surprised when he offers to give her a ride as far north as Oregon.

    "You a serial killer?"

"Might ask the same of you," he smiles.
"Stranger danger, you know."
"Up to you," he says, sipping his coffee, "Billy."
"Rita."
"Now we're not strangers."
"Doesn't really answer that whole serial killer question."

Billy simply shrugs and gives her a playful wink. His eyes – a pale blue – have a sort of milkiness off-set by his deep tan and the crow's feet that stretch out from his eyes. And now, not a half-hour after meeting this stranger she is sitting in the passenger seat of his battered Econoline-van, soaking in the smell of diesel and dust and cigarettes. The smell is so thick that when first goes to light a cigarette she is certain that the whole van is going to go up in flames. Perhaps mistaking her expression for something else he rolls down the window, and the breeze stirs his salt-and pepper hair as he squints at the road. There is no map beside him and he seems to chart a course by familiar or former landmarks; a string of forgotten towns that must for a constellation from Flagstaff to Albuquerque. Rita crumples her sweatshirt into a ball and tucks it between her shoulder at the window. It's far too loud in the van for music, let alone conversation, and the white noise of road hum and squeaking metal coaxes her to sleep.

When she wakes again Albuquerque has receded behind them by some unknown quantity of miles and minutes. It's the change in the road that wakes her—the smoothness of the highway giving way to rutted asphalt. She glances across at Billy now, trying to trace her thoughts back to the diner, and trying to shake off the disorientation of waking in a moving vehicle next to someone who she barely remembers meeting. A quarter of a mile down the road debris begins to appear, mixed in among the hardscrabble sage and spindly cacti. Unidentifiable rusting things are caught in the high, accusatory sun. A low-slung rambler comes into view, its white paint molting in thick flakes. Billy pulls up and parks in front of the detached garage, and before he even ratchets up the parking break a pair of black labs are circling the van – their coats thick with chalky dust and threads of ropey drool dangling from their muzzles.

As Rita steps down from the van she looks towards where a screen door has banged open. A tall man emerges from the house, his long bard nearly reaching his collar bone, his bald head shining.

"Don't worry," Billy says patting the dogs, "he's friendly. And I don't just mean the dogs. Daltry this is Rita. Rita Daltry."

Rita smiles cautiously as the two men shake hands, the dogs sniffing at her feet until Daltry calls them away, rattling a large wad of keys until he finds whatever he is looking for and plugs it into a padlock on the front of the garage. The doors open outwards like old barn doors, and the flattened dirt at their feet is carved by the rocks that have cut deep gouges in the earth where the door has caught them. At the front of the garage is a large motorcycle that, given the beastly size and chrome and dark leather, Rita assumes is a Harley. Beyond that there are makeshift tables – little more than sagging plywood propped up on old saw horses. Each table is crowded with odds and ends. As the lights overhead stutter to life she begins to decipher dozens of old appliances, mechanical and electrical things, most of which probably don't work anymore. The lines of the older machines betray a long gone period: substantial curving metal like the true lines of vintage cars. The look of machines that were intended to perch on countertops in the most modern homes is juxtaposed against the newer more angular plastic models. To Rita it's less appliance graveyard than archeological curiosity.

Billy pulls a pair of glasses from his breast pocket and perches them on his nose. The glasses give him a grandfatherly look as he makes a slow circuit around the table. Along the far wall a workbench is crowded with parts and tools and other unidentifiable detritus of someone who has horded machines and tools for years. Nothing hear matches, and the only order seems to be disorder.

"Looks a mess, don't it?" Billy asks without looking at Rita, "Guarantee Daltry here can find anything he wants in this place. Could probably even tell you the story of most everything in here."

"Here," Daltry says pulling back a canvas tarp, "this is what I was telling you about."

As the tarp is pulled back it reveals a pinball machine sides painted in bright yellows and reds. Stylized demons leer from the sides of the machine and the glass backboard is designed to match. No doubt generations of kids have leaned over the machine frantically tapping the little round buttons, for a moment drawn into a world composed only of the duration of a quarter and the clack of the flippers.

"Stuck relays?"

"Best guess. It's what made me think you might be interested. Pretty sure the problem is in the electrics. I could fix it up, but no way is it going to sell around here Better to ship it off to one of those places specializes in these sorts of things."

"Seems to be in good shape otherwise."

Rita jiggles the switch on an old blender, runs her hand along the frayed cord. She angles the gooseneck of a lamp and tries to imagine who it belonged to: a student bent over hours of homework, or a tired father endlessly paying bills. Maybe it illuminated the daily progression of paperwork that accumulates in domesticity. Billy and Daltry are haggling over the price of the machine in a way that seems comfortable and familiar, and is more than likely a game for the two of them. When they have settled on a price they begin to dismantle the thing and carry the discreet pieces out to the van, while Rita crouches by the garage doors speaking to the dogs in secret whispers; it's the first time she's been able to breath since she left.

The back of the van is already crowded with machines that Billy must have picked up in Albuquerque or Lubbock. AN antique coke machine lays flat on its back, held in place by its own weight. A scattering of power tools is heaped into battered cardboard boxes, cords coiled like sleeping snakes. The men are sweating now as they shimmy and angle the pieces into place and time them down with broad nylon straps. All of these things in the back of the van are things that she didn't notice when she first climbed into the van, and it's as if she sees them now for the first time as the van's suspension rocks precariously and shifts low over the wheel wells.

When the men are finished loading the machine into the van Billy slams the door closed and the two of them light cigarettes and sweat. They stand quietly as they smoke. Billy has taken off his glasses and put them back in his pocket and now he squints into the late morning. After a few minutes the men crush out their cigarettes and shake hands in truncated goodbye syllables slipping from their lips like smoke. And then Billy is guiding the van back onto the northbound highway.

"This is your job?"

"It's a living. I don't know if it counts as a real regular job type job."

Billy originally mentioned something about travelling across the states to pick up things he could fix and make money on, but it had been in her earlier state of exhaustion and that same exhaustion has settled in her temples now, fuzzing her vision. There was something about a military pension that he collected after serving twenty-five years in the Navy. Having retired several years ago. He'd said something about the way the road reminds him of the ocean. And for some unknown reason, either survival instinct or because she feels it would be impolite to fall asleep again she tries to stay awake – tries to keep the conversation going.

"You have a wife and kids?"
"Not that sort of guy."
"Guess not."
"You?"
"Ex-husband back in Austin. No kids."

The conversation slides into silence as they pass and repass the same cars for miles at a time and the road unwinds in front of them like a great black spool of ribbon that sometimes rolls straight through the desert and at other times bends awkwardly over the hills, folding back on itself in switchbacks that cause the engine to deepen its pitch until Billy finally downshifts. She is in and out of sleep. Sometime that first full day, after waking up again, she reaches over to where his pack of Marlboros shivers on the dashboard and draws one from the pack. Billy only nods and reaches down and pushes in the cigarette lighter with his knuckle. It's the first cigarette she's had in over five years, and the raw, burnt marshmallow taste of the thing coats her mouth and throat. She closes her eyes and lets the dappled red dots of sun create a curtain of her eyelids.

After several hours the sun paints the western sky tangerine as they cross into Utah, and by Cedar City that same sky is deep blue and edging towards black as the cooling breeze goose pimples Rita's skin. Her face is dry and warm and her arms are a newly sunburned pink.

At dusk Billy is pulling off of the freeway to fill the tank and then they stop briefly in a supermarket with cracked floors lackluster produce, and a harsh bright light that makes everything look startling real. Here Rita buys a few packs of cigarette sand the essentials that she's somehow forgotten: toothbrush, soap, deodorant. The handful of things in her basket look stark and mundane as she stands behind Billy noticing only the scraggly gray hairs on the back of his neck against the deeply skinned tan that is crisscrossed with creases from hours leaning over the steering wheel or peering intently into one machine or another.

The inevitable motel is stucco and equally lackluster; clinging to the streetlights and isolation of the highway. Billy parks in front of the small office and says he'll be back momentarily.

"Otherwise they'll feel sorry that you shacked up with an old doofus like me."

"That or you have plenty of cash."

"I cannot, ma'am, say that I am endowed with any particular thing that might make sense of this particular situation," he says as he shuts the driver's side door.

Inside the hotel room the AC churns decades of stale cigarette smoke stink, a smell that lord s over the narrow beds and the pink and green flecked carpet. The room itself is shabby in the same why that everything in the town seems shabby. Shabby in a way that betrays countless years of feet treading grooves in the carpet. Shabby from the countless cigarettes smoked and absorbed into the walls and blankets until no amount of laundry detergent or bleach will ever make the sheet truly clean again. The beds are well made with carefully smoothed floral comforter, and the whole room is cooled to nearly frigid. Billy sits at the edge of the bed closest to the door and retrieves a pint of whiskey from his duffle and pours a hefty slug into one of the plastic cups that have been left beside the sink. As he holds out the bottle to her she shakes her head.

"Think I'm going to shower first."

"Don't take all the hot," he says as he unlaces his work boots and drops them unceremoniously to the floor.

Rita closes the bathroom door and locks it behind her, although both door and lock are flimsy things. She can hear the TV come on in the other room, the sound merging with the air conditioner and the ceiling fan and the rush of the shower. She stands for a moment watching the water pool around the drain before stripping out of her sweat damp tank top and clammy jeans. Her body, o familiar, seems like a borrowed dress, like a hand-me-down from a forgotten self as she steps into the shower and lets the water soak into her skin washing away road dust and regret. She watches the water as it stutters over her stretch marks. Slowly, almost reluctantly she pushes the thin bar of hotel soap over her skin forcing it into a lather. The sudden cold of the water drags her from her daze and she finds herself sitting on the bottom of the tub. Reaching up she turns off the water and pulls herself up, drying off and dressing in yesterday's clothes. Her hair, free from its pony tail hangs in limp tendrils around her face.

    Outside, in the room, the TV casts a blue glow on the far wall and she can hear Billy snoring softly from the far bed. She pauses there in the doorway of the bathroom and weighs the decision to turn off the TV, but decides to leave it. As she lies down she can feel her wet hair soaking the pillow, but she is too tired to care. In the semi-darkness of the room she listens to the stranger's cartoon snore and tries to make sense of this wanderer, a man relegated to the road, who has decided to pick up a woman half his age in a diner without any expectation of anything more. There is nothing in him to indicate that he might be dangerous – and maybe she trusted him only on a semi-suicidal impulse. Ever since she left San Antonio, now well over twenty-four hours before, she promised herself that she wouldn't play thing safe or logical. There is no point in that now. Maybe it's a turn towards the ascetic.

She wakes again without realizing that she has been asleep with only a dim memory of lying I the bed waiting for sleep to come because sleep arrived before she had full settled into the foreign bed. As she eases into consciousness he looks around the room, half expecting the room in San Antonio. She expects John to be lying beside her, but even before she is fully awake, as she lingers in the no-man's land that stretches between sleep and wakefulness, she realizes that she isn't at home. The bed is slightly too cool and the comforter is slightly too scratchy. There is the stale scent of hotel soap and cigarettes. And then she is acutely aware of Billy as she spots him leaning against the frame of the open door smoking a cigarette. Just past him, outside, she can see the pale morning light straining over the torn paper hills of the horizon as the sun chases away the last of the night.

"Morning," Billy says over his shoulder.

"It looks that way," she says.

Billy shrugs and crushes out his cigarette in the oversized glass ashtray in the middle of the table. He is already dressed wearing a slightly different plaid shirt than he had been wearing the day before. Rita brushes her hair quickly, pulling at the snarls and snags in her hair with staticky snaps before sweeping it back into a ponytail that she knows will be loose and sloppy before the end of the hour. When she is ready she hands her room key to Billy and follows him out to the van where she stands smoking one of his cigarettes as he walks to the front office to return their keys. The van itself is cold from the desert night and she shivers down into her sweatshirt, huddling into herself as they pull onto the highway stopping only for gas station coffee.

Inside the little filling station convenience store Rita buys coffee as Billy tops off the tank. She thinks now of how easily he could leave her behind. She thinks of what it would be like to be stranded here in a place where she knows no one, without much more than the cash in her pocketbook. She wonders if she might even want him to leave her there. Or, perhaps she simply wants to disappear out the back door of the convenience store and go meandering down the back alleys of this anonymous town. There is a certain lightness in the disconnection; she is unmoored from any responsibility of past or future. But as she returns to the van she sets the coffee in the oversized cup holders and curls her fingers around her own cup, soaking in every bit of warmth that seeps through the cardboard.

There only real company is the number of semis that they leap frog up and down the highway; semis that displace walls of air that rock the van from side to side. They trace 15 north and she imagines that she can tell the locals by the way that they speed past in casually dented cars. She finishes a bag of chips from the gas station, crumples the empty bag, and tosses it onto the floorboards where it mingles with the other debris that has accumulated over hours on the road: empty pack s of cigarettes and soda cans, candy wrappers and convenience store bags. Within the hour signs for Yuba state park start to appear by the side of the road. They are squat brown signs with stark white lettering.

"Ever been?"

"Yuba?"

"You never been then we should stop."

She wants to get out of the van, but not as much as she desperately wants this trip to be more than a simple get-away. She wants to see something that she never would have seen otherwise. There is something about stopping here at the roadside state park that validates her leaving. It would add to the sense of adventure, she thinks. She would be able to say that at least she has seen something that she wouldn't have ever seen if she had stayed behind in San Antonio. Another sign comes into view and Billy begin to slow, downshifting as he eases along the off ramp and into the park itself.

A reservoir expands before them like an uneven mirror dotted with sailboats and inner tubes. Clusters of tents are perched on the pale, flat dunes and Billy coasts to a stop in the small parking lot. The white noise evaporates and now they are stuck with the sudden awkwardness of not having anything to say to each other. The engine ticks silently as Billy hangs his arm out the window, a curlicue of smoke making its way past the side mirror.

"People drive past places like this," she says.

"Lots of people drive by lots of places."

The soft breeze off of the reservoir dances her own cigarette smoke out the window in little waltzing movements and she opens the door and climbs down onto the asphalt. Heat radiates up off the blacktop in shimmering waves.

"Looks like there might be a better view over here," she says pointing to where the dunes rise and merge into the high pine trees.

"Go ahead," Billy says, "I'm a get twenty winks."

Rita follows a narrow dirt trail that emerges in a small shady area near a tent set on the high ground beneath the trees. Farther down, along the shore a man fusses with a hibachi while a woman in a lawn chair intermittently watches two young boys as they run and squeal and splash in the shallow water at the edge of the reservoir. The pale round bellies of the boys protrude over their brightly colored, matching swim trunks. She can't help but notice that the boys are only a few years younger than Alex as she steps down to the shore not far from where the boys are playing.

Stepping out of her shoes she lets the water lap timid waves around her toes and ankles. She imagines wading out there, farther and farther into the cool water, allowing it to envelope her an inch at a time, the level rising up her calves and thighs until eventually she would be weightless and the warm surface layer of water would give way to the deeper, cooler water just beneath. She could dive down deeper and deeper until her lungs burned and her muscles cramped. There in the thick darkness she would roll onto her back and look through the murk at the water shimmered surface as the water hemmed her in. Slowly, precisely, exhaled air would bubble from her throat, passing through her lips like unarticulated secrets and she would begin to sink until she was stored up behind the dam with the silt and silence; insulated by thousands upon thousands of gallons of water and upstream refuse caught there.

    Behind her on the shore the woman begins shouting to the boys, and the sharpness of her voice pulls Rita back to the present. She glances up and makes fleeting and accidental eye contact from the woman, causing them both to look away abruptly. Back at the van Billy is reclining in the driver's seat, his head tilted back. As she nears the parking lot she thinks of John, back at home, no doubt wondering where she's gone. She imagines him sitting at the kitchen table, having finally found the note that she left for him in the picture frame beside the bed, but, instead of dwelling she tries to chase these ideas away as she opens the passenger side door and climbs back up into the cab. Billy opens his eyes and grips the steering wheel to pull himself forward.

    "Good walk?"

Rita nods abstractly as she brushes the sand from the bottoms of her feet and shakes out her shoes before putting them back on. Billy turns the key and the van is alive again and they are slowly pulling back out of the spot. She knows that there, beyond the dunes, the two young boys are still splashing at the edge of the water. The man is still fussing with the hibachi and the woman is still looking up intermittently to check on the boys. In the middle of the lake a rowboat drifts, a man reclining in the bow with a fishing pool dipped into the water, where concentric circles expand from the invisible place where the line enters the water.

    They cross and re-cross the Snake River, following 86 as it cuts west, passing throw towns with names like Rupert, Heyburn, Mountain Home. The sky darkens and the clouds crumple into different shades of black and gray as the air becomes electric. After a few miles Rita rolls up her window and wraps the sweatshirt around her shoulders. She can't help but think back to the thunderstorms back in Texas. She thinks of the way that the small, fine hairs on her arms would begin to prickle in the hour or two before a thunderhead rolled across town. She thinks of the time that she had walked out onto the front porch with Alex in her arms. He had been little more than a year old then, but he was quiet and calm in her arms as they stood there watching the distant flashes and counting together in anticipation of the accompanying thunder. Even the slowest build and rumble and snap didn't startle Alex then as he looked up at her and twisted his head to the side to stare at the distant landscape. The lights had flashed of their faces and ephemeral shadows pirouetted on the flat landscape. John had thought that she was crazy for that, keeping a young child out in a thunderstorm. For nearly an hour Rita stood out there with Alex, and John stood behind them, just inside the screen door shifting nervously from foot to foot until they finally came inside.

 Now it is that same familiar electricity that prickles her skin and lets her know that the storm will start soon – a certain type of barometric pressure on her skin and she can't help but smile now. Soon enough the light crackles on the distant landscape in strobing, bright flashes, too far away for the thunder to reach them, and after another mile the rain seems to assault the van from all sides.

 "Some storm," Billy says.
 "How much more do we have?"
 "Another hour or so."
 The place, Caldwell, isn't far off of the freeway, and Billy pulls down a side street past boxy 1950s houses painted in light blues and pale greens. They pass house painted in off whites and barely grays, and finally he parks along the curb in front of a pale blue rambler with a scuffed front door. The rain has slackened by now, but the asphalt is a black mirror. A creosote smell lingers in the smell – the concrete has been dry for months at a time, she can

tell. The woman that answers the door is, as best as Rita can tell, about Billy's age and the two of them embrace in a casual way that makes Rita realize that she has never shared any form of physical contact with the man – not so much as a hand shake.

Billy introduces the woman as Nancy, an old friend, as the woman ushers them inside and takes their bags and sets them in a small office off the hallway before leading them into the kitchen where a man in a wheelchair stirs a steaming pot. The men shake hands affably and Billy introduces the man as his old Navy buddy, Paul. Rita can't help but wonder if it is the Navy that landed Paul in his wheelchair but she knows that it is something that she can't ask. She knows this just as much as she knows that it is unlikely that she'll learn the cause of the wheelchair anytime in the next twelve hours or so that they are in Caldwell. It's a place she may never see again, and people she may never meet again. Nancy hands her a can of cold beer and then they are all lighting cigarettes and talking as Paul putters about in the kitchen refusing any offer for help. The house itself is cramped; the space between furniture has been engineered to be just wide enough for Paul's chair to pass through, but otherwise the whole place is vaguely claustrophobic. Nancy wants to know how Rita ended up riding with Billy and Billy relates the story in his crisp, efficient sentences.

"Thought maybe you two were lovers," says Nancy.

"Jesus, Nan." Paul says.

"An honest question."

"It's all right," Rita smiles.

"You said you were from Texas?"

"Bad divorce."

"Best thing for it is to get away," Nancy says, "no kids?"

Rita shakes her head and the conversation moves through dinner and the history that Paul and Billy and Nancy shares extends far beyond Rita's reality. From what she can piece together the two men met in the Navy. The stories are from different ports and other sailors and it's difficult to track the fragmented memories, a jumble of forgotten names and barely remembered anecdotes. There are stories that pre-date even Nancy and she shakes her head as the stories begin, knowing the trajectory of the stories from the first word like an overplayed song. He has heard these stories however many hundreds of times and fills in the details that the men forget. Rita smiles and jiggles her foot under the table as she smokes and listens and smokes and listens. Each story that unfolds reveals a foreign truth, like a window she has glanced through by accident. It's a voyeuristic thing, and she can't help but wonder if this is simply the natural unfolding of life. Rita thinks of how nice it would be to exist only as a footnote in someone else's life –and wants desperately now to negate the world that she is a part of. If she is lucky, one day she will be only a half remembered anecdote told over cheap beer and cheaper cigarettes.

By midnight, empty beer cans have crowded out their elbowroom on the table and the four of them go on tapping cigarette ash into empty cans and talking and laughing too loudly until Nancy hazards a glance at the clock on the stove. It's late she says and they all agree, reluctant to end their evening, although the air in the kitchen is thick with exhaled blue smoke and eyelids are beginning to droop. It's probably time for them to all turn in, especially if Billy and Rita want to get an early start, although the thought of an early start is odd to Rita, who has no specific destination or deadline. Rita follows Nancy into the small office where the two of them work together to unfold the hide-a-bed and spread the sheets over the creased mattress. They work in quiet unison transforming what must be Paul's office into a guest room. There is a broad desk near the window that looks out on the backyard, and the desk is populated with knives and chisels and half-carved figurines and a small plastic pallet of paint.

"Can I get you anything else?"

Rita shakes her head and smiles as Nancy eases the door nearly closed, leaving only a gap that reveals a fraction of the hallway. It reminds Rita of the way that her mother used to leave the same type of gap in her bedroom door when she was still a girl; it's the same type of gap that she would leave after putting Alex to bed. In her underwear and a mostly clean T-shirt she crawls beneath the cool covers and wishes that she could stay – as if, even as an adult she could be adopted by these near strangers. The patchwork quilt stretches and ripples over her legs as she thinks of Alex far away, however many miles distant, in his room hating her, thinking of her, struggling to understand.

Even now, after the others have gone to bed the house is full of noises that carry through the crowded hallways like ghosts in a draft. She can hear Nancy out in the front room now making up a bed for Billy on the couch. There is the rustle and snap of blankets unfurling and Rita can hear the muffled murmurs of their voices, and, somewhere else, she hears what must be Paul maneuvering his chair towards a bed. She hears or imagines the spring squeak of a well-worn bed, and hears a door closed and hushed voices that are only mouse like mutterings in the walls. Rita turns towards the window and can tell that the storm has moved off, farther to the west, leaving behind only a light rain that scatters timidly across the windows.

When she wakes in the morning she can hear the others in the kitchen talking at a volume that tells her they are trying not to wake her. Maybe it is the smell of coffee and toast and eggs that has called her out of unconsciousness. She dresses and pulls the blankets from the hide-a-bed and folds them into uneven squares and stacks them on the edge of the mattress. As she pauses there by the door, trying to build up her nerve, she can hear the crinkle of a newspaper and for a moment is shocked that people still have newspapers delivered. When she steps into the hallway she can see the three of them sitting there over squares of newspaper folded into discrete sections. She watches, like a voyeur, the light way that Nancy lays her hand on Paul's shoulder as she pours his coffee. It reminds her of past less than a week old – and yet the emotional yells have begun to create callous between past and present self.

    It's after eight by the time they are carrying their bags out to the van. In the wake of the storm the morning is a luminous golden thing with high clear skies. Paul and Nancy watch from the porch as Billy fires up the van and the two of them wave one more time before the van edges away from the curb. Suddenly self-conscious of the silence Rita glances at Billy trying to find a particular beat in the steady silence; a moment to say something, if only she could think of something to stay. Beat after beat passes. Each times he is about ready to speak she loses her resolve. For a moment she thinks that she will tell him everything. She will tell him about her husband and her son. But she will not be able to answer the one real question.

    "You've known them a long time," she says finally.

    "Years."

    She wants to believe that beneath his truncated statement there is a current of memory that drags him back all the way to the time before Paul's accident, and now it sounds less real and more like the name of painting: Paul Before Chair. In the painting the two men stand side-by-side, grinning in their white Navy uniforms with their little round caps. But there are private things that she will never learn about them, and she knows now that there is an entire of cache of memories that belong to a person and that those memories, like the person themselves, can never be fully excavated, no matter how relentless the questioning. There is a part of each person, she thinks, that must remain an unknowable and unreachable Shangri-La. Some inaccessible place where the true-truth hides.

But now they are nearing the freeway and the silence will soon be overridden by road noise and so she takes the last few minutes to ask where they are headed. Somewhere north, Billy says, close to Seattle.

"Figure I might as well take you all the way there at this point."

Rita grabs the pack of cigarettes from the dash and punches in the lighter and stares at it until the little button pops back out. For a moment she wants to ask him why Seattle, and then she remembers that Seattle is where she told him she's headed. She wants to tell him now that he needn't bother. There is nothing in Seattle for her. She has never been. Before she can tell him, she realizes that she is beginning to rely on him too much, and it scares her. It seems too much like the same direction that she has come from.

Maybe there is some way in which she has unwittingly tied herself to this stranger, becoming connected in a way that she hasn't intended. It's too much like how she ended up with John in the first place, coasting through acquaintanceship to friendship and relationship. A relationship that was more steady gravitational pull than love-at-first-sight-Hollywood-Romance. And then the same gravitational pull locked her into John's orbit and she was stuck forever encircling him. For a moment she thinks that she will call John from the next gas station that they come to. She'll begin to apologize but he will insist, in his usual way, that he has already forgiven her.

    She will stand in a dry, sand-swept parking lot until John pulls up in his sensible sedan and parks in front of her, the car still running, the door hanging open as he wraps his arms around her. He'll hold her and tell her that he forgave her before she even hung up the phone. He forgave her as soon as he heard her voice. Alex is at home; John won't have been able to bring him. He would be unable to bear it. Once at home Alex will be harder to appease. But the only thing that matters now is that she is back and that they are together and that nothing can pull them apart now and all this craziness can be put firmly behind them. In a few years, maybe, they'll be laughing about the whole thing. A diminishing memory.

    But that won't happen. There is a filament stretching from her to John and Alex. A filament that has become stretched so taught that it is on the verge of breaking. The tension pulls against her heart, and she knows that as soon as it breaks she will be forever liberated. She simply has to be patient and wait for the days and miles to insulate her from her past. This is the hardest part she tells herself as she crushes out one cigarette and lights another.

"You all right?" Billy asks.

"Sure."

"Just checking, you seem, I'm not sure what the word is."

"Pensive?"

"Pensive. Thinking about something. Texas maybe."

"You know how it is," she says.

It's an empty phrase half shouted in the inside of a strange van in a place she never thought she'd be, and she realizes that he doesn't know and couldn't know, not truly, not ever. Thankfully Billy remains true to form, running at almost absolute Radio Silence. Outside the window the landscape begins to change, slowly, but definitely. There are more hills now, and the ranches and farms are dotted with pastured horses and cows.

"They say cows are sacred in India," she says.

"I ate burgers that seemed like a religious experience."

"I can see it," she says, "there is a nobility in them."

The van passes a rumbling semi and they follow the winding highway as it runs, at least for the time being, parallel to old railroad tracks. The day on the road has a familiar rhythm by now, like the grooves worn in the highway – abrade by hundreds of thousands of cars. Except for the changing license plates and scenery, they would be caught in the doldrums of nowhere America – the road stretching backwards and forwards inexorably. They stop only for gas and the routine is identical even if the names of the stations change. Billy stands at the pump arching his back, trying to pop the lowest vertebrate. Or he stretches over the hood of the van to scrape bugs from the windshield. Or he taps the over-full ashtray into an overfull garbage can. Inside the convenience store Rita scores the shelves for candy and beef jerky and chips. Buys the ubiquitous beer and cigarettes.

The desert landscape of Eastern Washington is somehow familiar: the same pickups and cowboy hats and gun racks. Washington, she'd thought, would be more metropolitan, comprised almost entirely of Seattle. Rita had always imagined that there would be more in the way of roadside attractions the types of places that you see in horror movies. Places out of tabloids that advertise two headed lizards and mummified Indian chiefs. But the places that they pass pale in comparison, and if Billy notices the signs or the billboards he ignores them except for the occasional snort or shake of the head.

A column of military trucks passes them, rumbling in mismatched tans and dark greens. The soldiers behind the high flat windows are anonymous in their helmets and uniforms. There's no doubt in her mind that some of the soldiers are veterans, although to Rita they look impossibly young, like kids playing soldier. It's only a few miles further and Billy pulls off of the highway and into the parking lot of yet another cheap motel. It's the first motel that hasn't been made almost entirely out of stucco and surrounded by depressed cacti. The single queen bed doesn't bother her either, even as Billy apologizes and insists – as if to reassure himself – that he will sleep on the floor. Rita considers, momentarily, turning on the TV but decides against it, hoping that the comfortable silence of the van will settle into the room, but even after hours of driving together in close proximity there is a pronounced awkwardness. They are no longer distracted by the unscrolling of the asphalt. There is no road hum to screen potential conversation. There is no anticipation of a destination other than sleep.

    Billy drains his glass, downing the last bit of whiskey that he has poured evenly into two glasses. Amber droplets ripple around the edge, as Billy squints and rubs his eyelids with grease cracked thumb and forefinger. He tilts the bottle and turns it slowly so that the unclaimable residue of alcohol chases itself around the inside of the bottle, and then, unceremoniously, he pitches it into the plastic waste basket with the thud of finality. She can tell that the end-of-day sobriety makes him acutely aware of his aching back and dry eyes.

"Saw a gas station a mile or so back up the road," he says.

"You want company?

Billy shakes his head and grabs his keys from the nightstand. She can hear his heavy boots on the metal stairs as he thumps down to the parking lot and then, after a moment, she can hear the engine of the van as it turns over, and headlights sway across the room as he backs out of the spot. It's the first time that she's been alone since Yuba – something like two days, forty-eight hours give or take. However, many minutes and seconds and half thoughts that adds up to; and here she is now alone in a foreign hotel room that smells only of loneliness. Rita opens her bag and spills the contents onto the faded bedspread. All of her clothes are dirty but she no longer cares. Even so, she tells herself that she will wash her meager items of clothing in the sink and hang them in the bathroom to dry while they sleep. In the morning she will pack the still damp clothes into her bag and drape them one at time over the back of her seat while they drive. There, the clothes will marinate in cigarette smell and exhaust.

Slipped into a side pocket of her backpack is her slim red wallet. She removes it now from the little zippered pouch and slides her ID from its plastic sleeve, wanting to reminder herself of the truth of herself. She wants to see her own image – not who she is now – she wants to see who she was before leaving. She reads the address on her license and tries to picture the house. There is the photograph that she pulled from the bedside frame before she left, and she runs a finger along the torn age. It's a picture taken over a year ago. Not long after leaving she tore John from the picture and let the fragment of him flutter out the window of a westbound Greyhound. She'd been afraid that the picture of him would stare at her accusatorily. But now it is Alex, who is gazing at something just off to one side of the camera that sears her heart. She struggles to recreate the moment in her head, but it is a moss covered stone, an idea that has blurred at the edges until the hard, definite lines have softened into uncertainty.

    Rita puts all of these things back into her bag and takes a towel from the bathroom and scribbles a note for Billy on the hotel stationary left with the Gideon Bible in the nightstand. This way he won't wonder where she's gone off to. When they first pulled up to the hotel she'd seen the rippling light of a pool on the high brick walls. Now she is there, a day's worth of captured heat breathing between her toes, as she slips out of her clothes and lays them over a lounge chair with her towel. Stripped to her underwear she wades out into the cool water, until she is sweeping her arms in broad, even strokes, her feet kicking lightly as the bottom of the pool slopes away from her: four five six feet. At the deep end of the pool she exhales until all that is left in her lungs is an aching tightness. She bounces softly against the textured bottom of the pool, her hair tendriling around her like pale smoke and the chlorine stinging her eyes. She wants the weight of the water pressing down on her now – the unforgiving insistence. Tomorrow she will step out of the van at the next gas station and she will disappear, leaving Billy waiting there for fifteen or twenty minutes until he finally ducks inside the convenience store to check for her. He will wait by the ladies' restroom until a stranger emerges and looks at him with suspicion. And then he will return to the empty van and know that she is gone and the pain he feels will be a fraction of what it might have otherwise been.

Acknowledgements

Thank you to Jil, partner in crime and love of my life, who indulges me. To Caden, our daughter, who reminds me of the simple joys in life. And to my parents, who I am lucky enough to think of not only as parents, but as friends. To all of my family, both by blood and by bond of friendship.

Thank you to Hollins University, for letting me muddle through an MFA (especially Cathy Hankla, Liz Poliner, and David Huddle, Rase McCray, and Adam Dorris). Thank you to Seattle's Writers In The Schools program for letting me sneak into one of the most talented groups of peers I could ever have wished for – you are people on a sacred mission. Thank you to Ms Eick, at TOPS K-8, for letting me learn to be a better writer from both you and your students. Thank you to the Richard Hugo House for providing space for myself and all of the other emerging writers in Seattle.

Thank you to every publication that ever took a chance on publishing my work.
Thank you to Unsolicited Press (especially Rubie and Summer), for all your support and advice and thoughtful editing.

And thank you, thank you, thank you, to those writers who inspired me. I raise a glass to (in no particular order): Milan Kundera, Don Delillo, Cormac McCarthy, Richard Bausch, Michael Ondaatje, Charles D'Ambrosio, Peter Rock, and so many more.

And finally, finally, thank you to those who read and imagine and believe.

Made in the USA
Charleston, SC
12 January 2017